Rick Labour
ricklabour@gmail.com

The notching of the belt
An erotic autobiography

By Rick Labour

NOTE:

All events in this book are based on

true events that took place in my lifetime.
Names, places and dates have been changed to protect the innocent from undue scrutiny. Any similarity to real world persons does not guarantee involvement. Reader discretion is highly advised, book contains many adult themes and situations.

Copyright © 2020

All rights reserved.

ISBN:

ISBN-13:

This book is dedicated to the very people that have made my life what is today.

A heartfelt thank you to those who have made this erotic autobiography possible.

Every notch forever changed me.
Whether for good or evil I shall never know. Each story shall live on in these pages.

To my loving supporting wife I owe my life itself.

Finally, L.S - your truly a disciple of Christ.
Sorry you found me too late.

CHAPTER ONE
Raw Desires

"I'll suck your dick for a cheeseburger!" She proudly proclaimed as I stood, aghast, at the counter. For a moment my mind was blank as I tried to comprehend what I had just heard. I stood frozen in front of the cashier, panicked, face bright red in embarrassment as a single bead of sweat rolled down my forehead. The cashier looked back at me, caught just as off guard as I, as eager to know the answer as everyone else in earshot. In just a single turn of phrase the understanding of somethings worth changed dramatically. I went from a lucky teenage boy to a lowlife pervert in the tick of the clock. I needed to make a choice then and there. Lord knows if I made the right one.

That moment changed my life forever. Whether for the better or the worse I'll never know. I'm far from ashamed at what I've managed to accomplish in just a short interval in my life but I am by no means cocky or proud. All of the events in the book really happened to me - the glory and the shame. The submissiveness and the dominance. The horror.

    I write this book to educate and hopefully guide those brave enough to finish down a brighter path. Any laughs or sexual arousal are a happy byproduct of my wisdom. Intertwined in the erotica are life lessons I've suffered greatly for. Don't suffer like I did: take my word for it. I can assure you the pain can be all to real. The nightmares have not gone away even a decade later. To call this journey of sexual discovery a walk in the park would be and injustice. I risked my health and safety with every notch. In times I endangered the safety of my friends as well. Weigh the risks before taking any actions. There is more to life then getting your dick wet, much much more.

    So… How *did* I end up in that situation?

    It had all started about a year before, in the heat of the summer. I was on my way to my best friend Mark's place to play some video games and just relax. It was way too hot to do anything outside, so it felt like as good a plan as any for the day. To my surprise, as I approached the door I was greeted by none other then Mark's sister, Emily.
    Apparently she was expecting me.

    Emily had a decent body, 5'2 not fat but a little on the chubby side. Her shoulder length brown hair blew ever-so-gently in the wind as her deep emerald eyes seemed to gaze into the depths of my very soul. The cute grin across her face told me she was up to no good.

"Happy to see me?", she asked.

"Uhhh... sure... I came over to play some games with Mark, is he around?"

Her hand reached out and grabbed mine. " He's still asleep but there's something I want to show you downstairs before he wakes up," she said, seeming excited and somewhat nervous. She reached and took my other hand in hers. I couldn't help but blush.

"What's downstairs", I inquired having the curiosity get the better of me.

"Come on . I'll show you", she said trading my hand for the doorknob and guiding me inside. She led me through the house to the basement door. A very crudely drawn sign haphazardly taped to it read, " Raw Desires - Club members only" in bright red capital letters. She turned the knob and we began our descent. Shutting the door behind me I could hear others talking below as I took my chance to watch Emily's ass bounce as she went down the stairs. At least I would not be alone with her, who knows what trouble we could get into?

As we entered, the room was filled with a sense of joy. There was bubbly laughter and nervous giggling. I was the only one in the room that had no clue what he had walked into. Up until that point in life I want to say I was a pretty innocent teenage boy. I had never done *anything*. Never watched an adult movie or even seen a woman nude. That all changed.

There was a total of six of us, three boys and three girls. At that point I realized I was the missing piece of the puzzle. This wasn't any ordinary club. I had just grabbed a seat and felt lips pressed against mine. It shocked me and I blushed like a ripe cherry tomato. I barely had the time to close my eyes as Emily planted a nice juicy kiss on my lips.

" WOW", was all that could escape my lips after that special welcome. The other members couldn't help but laugh at my obvious inexperience.

After the giggling died down the kissing started. This was moving too fast. My innocence was ripped asunder by ideas and acts we were too young to understand. She didn't just want me in the club, she wanted *me*. I went down those stairs a boy and came up a man. It had completely contradicted everything I had been told up to that point in life. I was told from a young age that sex was for marriage and only if you're in love. What was to be a lazy day of relaxation turned into something you only hear about in the threads of a sex forum or recollections in the back of a dirty magazine.
Not my worst Thursday afternoon.

There ended up being a few more meetings after that. Who was I to complain? Everything in that way of life was new to me and I was down to sample what life had to offer. I had no complaints about Emily and she kept coming back for more so I can only assume the feeling was mutual. She tried her best and hey, at the time, she *was* the best I ever had. There was some jealousy amongst members so the group grew apart. Luckily that did not put any distance between me and Emily.

Truly, it was much more enjoyable getting down without sets of eyes looking you over as you did the deed. She had grown quite fond of me, but I just could not feel the same way about her. The idea of having my best friend as my brother-in-law seemed like a disaster waiting to happen. I kept emotionally distant, savoring both relationships as long as possible. We were just horny teenagers trying to get by any way we could.

Everything had gone pretty smooth until I gave her a black eye.

I can explain- please don't rush to condemn me. It was a literal knee jerk reaction in the heat of the moment. The basement, our secret hook-up spot, was the perfect place to not get caught. For some reason it never aroused suspicion and no one asked why we were down there. The room was not the cleanest, nor the most comfortable, but it did offer seclusion from the top of the stairs. A safety net, so to speak, where even if someone came rushing down the stairs full speed you still had enough time to hide your actions.

Well on that particular day she had me in her mouth trying her best to make me feel good. Those innocent dark green eyes stared up at me as her head bobbed up and down. Her tongue swam around me and continued to bring me closer and closer to flooding her throat. She began to speed up, her sucking more intense by the second. She was focused and determined to get me to bust, I could hold back no longer. The muscles in the pit of my stomach tightened as I prepared to let it happen. That was when I got caught in her braces.

I can honestly say I am good at handling extreme amounts of pain. Car accidents, tattoos, burns- you name it I can pretty much handle it. Put my dick in a can opener, though, and I'm gonna react. It hurt so bad I ripped it from her mouth and thrust forward again jabbing her right in the fucking eye with a fully erect ejaculating penis. I felt bad, but kept erupting all over her face as she started to cry. Once you start you just can't stop so I stood there unleashing everything all over her. In too much pain and joy to move.

I apologized but that wasn't good enough. I'm standing there, holding my damaged member that is now slightly bleeding as I hear the door open.
"What the fuck is going on down there?" her mother yells as we are hiding in the back corner.
"She tripped and fell in the dark, shes fine, we will be up soon!" I shouted, praying that it sounded believable.
The door slammed shut. I was too scared. Like that level of fear that you may actually shit your pants. What would have happened if she would have came down and saw me standing there over her daughter, dick in hand, Emily painted like a jizzcasso on her knees crying and holding her face? That was a little too close.

It became rare that we hooked up after that. We only went at it when both of us needed a good release. One day we needed it was in the middle of July. We were at a private pool, the home of one of Mark's uncles. The water truly was refreshing, but meant nothing compared to the tall cool glass of water I was sharing the pool with. It was just Mark, Emily, and I that day. Usually more friends came along but all were too busy to attend today. This was exactly what we were hoping for. We spent a few hours playing Marco Polo before Mark had had enough. He got out, hopped on his bike and headed for home. That left me and Emily all alone in the pool with no one in the house either. This was exactly what we were hoping for.

    Believe it or not, watching someone in a bathing suit for a few hours can get your motor running. During the game of Marco Polo we had made sure to cop a feel every time we caught one another. We picked a spot in the low section right in front of a water jet. I bent her over the side, letting her tits rest on the pool's edge. Emily was wearing a one piece swimsuit, easy enough to slide aside and slide up on in. The heat of her sex combined with the cool rushing water made sensations a man only dreamed about. I came faster then I'd like to admit, remaining inside waiting for round two. I looked around as her fuck tunnel squeezed me awaiting more pounding and hopefully a second load. The birds were chirping, squirrels were running around the yard, a butterfly flapped around the edge of the pool.
    Mark was watching us.

    I never knew how long he had been there. Whether he had forgotten something and came back, or whether he had set up a sting operation I knew not. If he didn't know I was involved with his sister before… he sure knew then. As I met his eyes he turned around and left. Round two wasn't going to happen. I felt shame for the first time, not a pleasant feeling. Mark and I seemed to get closer after that in a weird way. He went out of his way to say I was going to marry his sister more then once. To him, becoming my brother in law was a great idea. He knew me better then anyone else. I was already part of the family. That last step would make it official.

   I had to do some serious thinking on whether or not that was the path I really wanted to go down. Was this my destiny? Would I ever find love? If sex and love are independent from one another then what can love really be? I definitely had more questions then I had answers. We were both just young stupid teenagers who, in retrospect, are very lucky we did not become parents. Luck was on our side and we kept just safe enough to not conceive a child.

   Here we are, back at the moment the book all began. I stood there with all eyes upon me who were within earshot when she had made the offer of oral sex for a cheeseburger.
   "I would like a cheeseburger for the lady," I said, and turned to Emily," Thank you for the offer, but this one's on me".
   We left there hand in hand but never had relations again. In a few words she had reframed sex from something priceless to something worthless. If someone was willing to please me for the cost of something on the value menu, then it was probably not

that good. The innocence was gone, replaced by years of nightmares about having my dick bitten off.

Once I stopped seeing Emily the relationship between her brother and I grew more sour by the day. What once were happy dreams of being my actual brother were now feeling of anger from being rejected. To be honest, in the grand scheme of things he took the separation the worst. We kept it alive for a few more years, keeping distant and seeing if time could heal the wound. The wound had become infected- amputation our only available recourse. We have not spoken in over a decade and perhaps that is for the best.

If I were to pick up an adult book and it began this way, I don't quite know how I would react. This isn't your typical adult novel filled with anything raunchy that comes to mind, this is an autobiography based on what really happened to me. Life isn't perfect and some stories in this novel are better then others. I thought it proper to keep things with little description as possible in this chapter due to the fact that it involved myself and others before we turned eighteen. Chapter two and beyond is all eighteen plus, however- so sit down and clear your afternoon. You're not going to want to put this down once things get going.

CHAPTER TWO
Just not good enough

Soon after Emily and I stopped seeing each other I needed some time to clear my head. I ended up staying single for over two years as I tried to understand the true meaning of love. Senior year of high school rolled around and I decided to give it another shot. I hoped that I had just grabbed the short straw and gotten the crazy one right out from the get go. It could be smooth sailing from here on out.

I set my sights on a friend of a friend. Her name was Scarlet and she was also a senior. She had her hair dyed dark red and her brown eyes were so dark that they were almost black. A thin smile drew you away from her very pale skin. She had legs that went on for days and a narrow waist. Her bust and booty were small but she seemed like a wholesome girl with a good personality. She was goth and dressed in all black ninety-percent of the time. This was my first time actually being the one to ask a girl out, so a strong sense of fear was firmly upon me as I asked her. Thank god she said yes.

In retrospect, I can't quite understand why I was so fearful of being rejected. Although she was not ugly, she was far from the prettiest girl I had ever met. She had very few friends and did not really fit into any clique that I knew of. At my school, girls like her were few and far between. She was the kind of emo/goth girl that everyone had their own stereotypes about. She listened to sad music, wore all dark makeup- that sort of thing.

Deep down, I felt that maybe she just wanted to be accepted. Perhaps a sense of belonging or compassion would snap her out of it and that love could be the cure to this behavior. The more I got to know her, the more I understood why she acted this way. Her parents had divorced when she was little and blamed her. The father turned to drinking, the mother to harder drugs. It was not the type of environment any child should have to grow up in.

At the time, I felt like the luckiest man in the world. She had accepted me with open arms and set a date and a time for us to hang out. I was tickled pink at the possibility of having a normal relationship for once in my life. Something like you see in a happy movie. Just two people spending time together in love was all I was after. I had very high hopes that this was going to be a great year.

Time seemed to fly by as I waited to spend time with my newest companion. I was excited to finally have someone to spend time with and, if I was lucky, maybe get a kiss at the end. My first kiss that was the way I wanted- not just a quick peck and then a hand tugging at my zipper but a sweet and passionate locking of the lips that would make my heart flutter.

    As I arrived at her house my heart was beating out of my chest. I climbed the stairs and tryied to be calm as I rang the bell awaiting what would greet me on the other side. She opened the door and my jaw dropped at the gothic princess standing before me. She had really gone all out and I was truly appreciative she had done so. A very revealing all black tank top, a short black miniskirt loaded with lace, and thigh-high catholic school socks brought me to full attention. Her makeup must have taken her at least an hour. She looked flawless.

    Luckily, she took the lead and invited me in or else I would have stood there all day lost in my own imagination. Inside it was silent. We were alone .
    "So, do you wanna watch a movie?" she asked.
    "Sure, that sounds like a great idea," was my reply. I didn't know at the time how great of an idea that really was. After a few minutes we decided on an old horror movie and cuddled up on the couch. To this day I cannot tell you the plot. The image on the screen hadn't mattered, she was the one with my full attention. I held her closely, my breath gently flowing over her neck as my hand slid ever so slowly up and down her side. Her pale face turned pink. Suffice to say she also did not give two shits about the movie.

    I had arrived with the hopes of having some genuine dialog but alas, squeaks and moans were the only sounds that left that couch. After twenty minutes of side gliding I started to make my move. My hand began to wander farther and farther up her side and began to glide over her breast. They may not have been the biggest, but they were perky and her nipples were super sensitive. She hadn't worn a bra so my hand fully explored the tenderness of her skin and the outline of her areola. Gentle moans escaped her lips as she was given more intimate attention. I decided to press my luck even further and ventured south. Slowly moving my way to her soaked black lace panties. The skirt she wore did nothing to defend her virtue. We repositioned so I could give her nipple a flick with my tongue. She shivered with delight.

    The foreplay was nothing short of torture for her. She was writhing as my lips gave a gentle suck and my hand dragged across her sex at a snail's pace. She slid down the skirt and underwear, forcing my hand to her thigh. Her breathing quickened as I slid my hand up and down, continuing to tease. I was barely touching her sopping wet mound, driving her further and further into madness. She had waited this long, why not longer? Even with her young glistening pussy exposed to the world, a tempting target, instead I slid up her chest and copped another feel. She quickly grabbed my arm, unamused by my excessive teasing, and placed my hand on her pussy. Good things in life are worth waiting for, my hands are no exception. Cautiously I slid in a finger all the way down to the bottom knuckle. A long deep exhale escaped her as I slid in. Not even a minute had passed and I could tell she was close to finishing, her hand tightening around my wrist as I fingered her.

It was time to go in for the kill. I slid not one, but two fingers inside her. Her legs locked shut and she squeezed the couch cushions and my wrist with all god gave her. That one thrust was enough and she had came. All that lead up and she finished in a matter of seconds. I wasn't about to stop so soon so I withdrew my fingers from her and started rubbing her swollen clit, dancing around her love button 'til she shook so hard she fell off the couch. I didn't even have time to ask if she was alright, she hopped right back up and we went at it again. Her legs were spread wide apart and the heat coming off her womanhood was intense. Her leg was pressed up against me and my cock was aching from being pressed to the inside of my pant leg. I decided to give her one more thrill before asking for anything in return.

The movie was playing the credits as I began to bring her to climax again. She lifted her hips and rocked them as I raked my fingers inside her. She reached up to grab my hand but I just kept going.
"Yes! Yes! Yes! Oh god!" she chirped as I felt her squirt all over my hand. Her juices gushed between my fingers as her cunt spasmed around them trying desperately to stop my hand from moving. I ceased and held her, pulsing cunt and all. She was shivering, her legs were jelly, her face fully flushed. I had done my duty as a man. She looked me in the eye and I leaned in to give her my first real kiss, one that I initiated. Her mouth was hot and her pussy quivered on my fingers still inside her as we locked lips. I

gently slid my fingers out. I hadn't even the chance to wipe them off when I heard the lock click on the front door just several feet away. My face turned to my new lover. She had heard it, too.

Those few moments felt like they went by in slow motion. In a seamless move, she got up, grabbed her clothes, and dashed to the other room. I had just enough time to swap seats on the couch to cover the newly formed stain. A second later, the door flew open. Her mother on the other side. Carrying groceries she was completely oblivious of my existence on the couch as she made a beeline for the kitchen. As she came back through she jumped as she saw me.
"Hi, there. I'm Scarlet's friend, Rick. Do you need any help carrying in the groceries?" I asked praying that she did not notice the absence of her daughter, the clearly visible erection running down my pant leg, or the fragrance of freshly drilled pussy wafting around the room. Luckily, she did not need my help so I got to sit and relax as my blood returned to the rest of my body.

As her mother returned from the second trip to the car, Scarlet reappeared. Her outfit had changed to something more modest including a bra to hide her swollen teats. A quick goodbye and I made my departure, not even staying for the goodbye kiss that I was hoping for. I had gotten one during the act so I chalked that up as a win. Having gotten away with our fondling by the thinnest of hairs we thought it best to not have fun at her place again. Frankly, her mom scared me and I did not want to poke the bear anymore then I already had.

We knew we had to sneak out, but where to go? What spot would have no one around, be kinky, and appeal to her dark nature? Only one place came to mind- the graveyard.

We fell pretty quickly into a simple routine. We would wait until after midnight and then I would sneak over with the family truck and grab her. After that, we headed to the graveyard and parked far enough away from the road that we could not be seen by passersby. All that was left to do was get in the backseat and start having some fun. It was a full size SUV and we had the seats folded down so we could really spread out. We kept the windows cracked ever so slightly so that they would not fog in the chill of the night. Time and time again I would leave her in a puddle of her own satisfaction and I was left high and dry due to one reason or another- "It's getting late, I should probably get home", or "I'm too tired after all you've done, I can get you next time though!"

Although I highly enjoyed what I was doing I wanted more than to just be a piece of meat to her. She was always kind and friendly to me but I felt like she did not like me the same way I liked her.

Whether I am like most men I cannot say. I find it very rude for a man to pump and go, leaving the woman sitting there wanting. Women should cum first and men should come second or not at all. Over time though this started to wear on me. Was there something wrong with me ? I know she was inexperienced and pretty nervous about having fun in general. That I can definitely work with and am willing to put the time and effort in to make sure everyone is comfortable with what is going on. A man can only drive away with blue balls so many times before he can't take it anymore. I had no normal relationships to look back on to see if this was the way things were supposed to be or not. From what I had heard, it was customary to make the guy happy by the third date but I had no real world data to back that up. We had hooked up in the truck a dozen times. Truly, that felt like overkill so I decided enough was enough and I had to take a stand.

At this point, I still was not quite sure what love was. I knew I was making her feel good in ways that I dreamed would be reciprocated. We are talking twelve, count' em twelve, thirty-minute moan and groan sessions of my tongue and her labia going toe-to-toe. That number doesn't even count our first "date" (if you can really call it that) on that couch. This girl may be the reason I have arthritis today after giving her so many rub downs it would make your head spin. Was I an asshole for wanting something in return? She was too nervous to give a blow job, this did not upset me as my last encounter had me nervous and mentally scarred. She had tried once or twice to give me a an old fashioned but that did not get very far either. There was only one option left it seemed: I was going in, or I was shipping out.

The night had come, it was our thirteenth meeting in the graveyard. We went to our usual spot after I picked her up. As always, her body knew what it was in for. Her pussy was now always wet upon arrival, almost trained. This saved some time. My strategy had to be severely altered. Usually I went right to the goal but tonight I just danced around the forty yard line. She was squirming and getting impatient. I had her right where I wanted her. I stopped, sat up, and waited for her to sit up too. Her confused look was expected, I could not blame her. Most guys don't just abruptly stop giving you attention unless something is the matter.

"Tonight is the thirteenth time we have been physically intimate in the back of this truck. I want to make it clear that I need attention too. Although I enjoy making you feel good I cannot keep leaving here with blue balls every night. You have a choice to make, you can figure out some way to make me cum with your mouth or hands, OR, we can go to a nearby park and have sex. Your choice"

She gave me an evil glare and said I was being unreasonable. The way I saw it was the other way around. As she sat there with her nipples sharp enough to cut glass and the faint odor of sex drifting around it was clear she was enjoying what I had done. Before I had stopped I had brought her close to an orgasm, not close enough to accidentally finish but another ten seconds and the back of the truck would have been soggy.
"Well, I'm not going to suck you off to try and win your approval and I'm not going to be able to jack you off," she said.
"So does that mean we are headed to the park, or

am I headed to your house to drop you off?" I fired back not missing a beat.

A few moments passed. "I guess we can go to the park. Just don't cum inside me," she said with a grin across her face. I was finally gonna cum for once.

We got to the park I had in mind and walked to a jungle gym far off the beaten path, It was old, not the popular one all the kids used, but it was all ours. As we walked up she asked, "Is it going to hurt? I'm a virgin."

Her question caught me off guard a bit. This was good news and bad news and I was not one hundred percent sure of the answer at the time. "You're so wet I will surely glide right in and you'll be fine. Might be a little bit of blood but you'll survive. It will be over before you know it."

This answer seemed to put her at ease as I picked her up and sat her on a part of the jungle gym that was pretty close to dick height. I felt a sense of pride that she had chosen me (although begrudgingly) to pop her cherry. Even to this day I feel very honored to have been her first.

It felt like walking out of prison and walking to the electric chair all at the same time. The cool of the night was the only thing keeping my sweat at bay. My throat was dry. My hands shook as I ran them up and down her thighs and gazed down at her sex. My bulge was sore, balls full to near bursting levels. I had to keep my cool or else I was going to flood her womb with seed. The arousal of the situation combined with the fear of getting caught made me afraid I was going to finish earlier then desired. I did not want to disappoint her as it was her first time. I teased her for a minute by gently gliding the head up and down the entrance of her slit making sure she was ready for me. Her juices ran down my shaft and I made it slick all the way to the base. I took a deep breath and ever so gently glided all six and a half inches up inside her.

Something was wrong, very wrong. Virgins were supposed to be tight and have a hymen, right? I had gone in all the way to the base but could not feel anything in the form of resistance. I withdrew to see if I was the problem only to be able to see my pulse in the vein on the side of my rod. I was as ready as I was ever going to get but there was no sensations coming from inside her. This went on for about a minute before I gave up hope and pulled out. I was no closer to orgasm than when I had started and still needed to cum. I asked her if I could finish on her tits and, thank god, she agreed. It wasn't much of a target to aim at, but more than I deserved after that performance. After maybe a minute of good firm tugging I unleashed torrents of cum upon her. She was shocked at how much had come out and so was I. It was enough to cover her entire chest and then some. I gave her my underwear to clean up but even after that she smelled strongly of my penis perfume.

We walked back to the car in silence and drove her home without a word. My mind was swimming in an ocean of confusion and doubt. I tried talking to her the next day but her responses were short and distant. Did she regret going all the way? Had I been the bad guy all along and was this all my fault? Did I throw away a good thing by putting my needs ahead of my partner's? To these questions I have no answers.

    Some part of me still longed for a physical relationship with her even though I knew we were physically incompatible. I asked her to be my girlfriend. She declined the offer. I told her I wanted to be with her. She said no. I prodded and got my answer. It was not the fact that we had had a less than desirable night on a playground with some awkward penetration, as foolish me had assumed. It was because of who I was. Turns out she was embarrassed of me. She told me she would feel shame and embarrassment if she told her friends she was involved with a guy like me. To be honest, that hurt more because it meant I didn't fuck up, I *was* the fuck up. Being the fat kid in school I got a lot of mean comments chucked my way, but that cut deeper than anything anyone else had ever said to me.

    Did I deserve it? I'd like to think not, but who can honestly say. All I knew was now that the truth was out I was gonna make sure everyone knew my side of the story too. I made sure each and every one of her friends knew that we had fucked. Everyone learned what she did and how she led me on. The nights in the graveyard were no longer just our little secret. I made sure everyone she knew had intimate knowledge of her cavernous vagina. My go to phrase, "'twas like a bowl of lukewarm mashed potatoes I only wish had more lumps", got used many a time. Some would say I was an asshole for doing so but in hindsight, someone who is an 'embarrassment' may also in fact be an 'asshole' as well.

    Word of this spread to Scarlet and she did not take it on the chin. What did she expect me to do after being treated like that, just curl up in a ball and cry? Fuck no. By being a monster you tend to create a monster. Be honest from day one and you have nothing to fear for the truth is out there and well known. Simple concept to wrap your brain around. It took her a while to get over the whole ordeal. She spent some time being depressed, some time being suicidal, but after a while she sort of leveled out over the long run.
    Things turned out alright for her in the end, I guess. She ended up getting engaged to a man who is very nice but has apparently never made her orgasm. How would I know this? I talked to her after over a decade of silence and she came right over to be satisfied. We hooked up once, then parted ways again. This is the sweet nectar of karma that keeps me going in the dark times, knowing that if you fuck me over the universe will make your life even shittier then you made mine.

    That girl had lead me down some dark tunnels and I was trying desperately to find a way out. I started lashing out in bad ways. I was an asshole to a lot of people and lost most of my friends. The girls who used to talk to me all dried up and stopped doing such once they saw what I could do to someone that fucked me over. All in all I was angry most of the time, full of angst. This anger lead me to a parking lot roughly a twenty minute drive from home. The people there were angry too and were bonded by their anger. Society had cast them out just as it had me. This was no ordinary social gathering, this was a meeting for the men who wear the pointed hats and dress in all white robes. I had done all the research I could online and these people and I had a lot in common. Perhaps they would accept me for who I was. They were angry at the world and at least they had someone to blame.

    As a child, I had several negative experiences with people of color that left me wondering. All were random acts of violence from people I didn't even know. I had never met them before but they could punch me in the face because I was white and they were not. In the town where I grew up, if you were white you were the minority and the target of unjust persecution. At age eight a group of boys tried to drown me in a public swimming pool. They took turns slamming me into the water and laughing as I swallowed more and more. I saw my mom running up to stop them as I began to lose consciousness. As soon as she got me on dry land I started vomiting water. We grabbed our things and never went back there.

    At age ten a boy tapped me on the shoulder and as I spun around shot me in the forehead with a slingshot at point blank range. He also could not stop laughing as as blood ran down my forehead from the penny he had launched at my skull. Luckily I at least remembered seeing this guy up the street once and the police found him and took him to juvenile hall for a couple months. Never spoke to him before and never did anything to cause him harm. He told the cops, "I did it because I thought it was funny". I'll tell you right now I wasn't fucking laughing.

    If that wasn't enough, I have been jumped twice by gangs of high-schoolers, all black kids. Once was in an alley just out of sight from the road, the other was just outside my home. I had walked over to the pizza shop which was only seventy two feet from my front door. Walking back I got jumped. No idea why, other than I was the white kid. They ran off before I could get inside to find reinforcements or something to fight back with. They laughed as they ran away, knowing I could not catch them even if I wanted to. I did not find that nearly as funny as they did.

    So there I was, sitting in my car in this parking lot, my mind going a thousand miles a minute trying to figure out what I should do. The lot filled with rusty old trucks with patriotic bumper stickers that displayed their strong support for the second amendment and dislike for abortion. There were old men as well as young, all standing around shooting the shit before the meeting. No women that I could see, not that I expected any. All my life I've based my decisions off of two main principles, honesty and logic. Even though it was made abundantly clear throughout my young life that some people of color hated me because of my skin, it did not mean that all of them did. These men all agreed that all black people were bad, a statement that I knew, deep down in my heart could not be true. To join their ranks would have meant I would have to abandon not only honesty, but my logic as well. I could not bring myself to do that for surely not all black people are bad. One was the president for fuck's sake.

    I had made my decision that the life waiting for me out in that parking lot was not one I wanted to be a part of. I started my car, drawing the attention of the group chatting away. I got given the good ole stink eye from a few of the old timers, that stare of a southern gentleman that says, "Go on, now! Git!!!"

    As the view of the lot disappeared from my rear view mirror I knew I had made the right decision. Whatever path that would have taken me on could in no way compare to the path that I walk upon to this day. Love is a choice and so is hate. Your decision to hate someone or something determines who you are just as much as when you choose to love.

    Hard to believe that eight years later I stood at the altar awaiting my African goddess of a bride to march up and give me her hand in marriage. That's right, a woman of color turned out to be my soulmate. Love had truly overcame the hate in my heart in ways I would never have expected. My groomsman, an immigrant who came here in the back of a mattress truck, smiled and clapped as we walked up the aisle. Your consciousness directs you to decisions which, at your own discretion, lead you down paths of near infinite opportunities. Choose not to limit yourself with hate but expand your horizons with love. Such choices will truly make this world a better place.

CHAPTER THREE
What life has to offer

    Senior year had come to a close and all of the high school drama was now a thing of the past. I was finally free. The world was at my fingertips, my mind full of not only hopes and dreams but fair amounts of self-doubt. Every morning I would see myself in the mirror and wonder exactly who was staring back at me. Who was I? Was I a man deserving of love? Was I truly even a man at all?

    When someone tells you you're an embarrassment and not deserving of love, it makes you wonder why they said that. Was I really too ugly to be taken as a serious partner, let alone mate? I wanted to prove to not only myself, but to the world, that I was worth something. For some reason I felt the need to show I was worthy of basic human kindness and decency. I came up with a plan to solidify my bravado. Fifty stuck out as the number I needed to reach to once and for all know, deep down, that I was not a failure. Fifty women had to fall on my sword.

Discretion was a top priority in this endeavor. I did not *need* to know your name. Your identity is none of my concern. My name? If pressed for it I would give it without hesitation. Even though they knew my name, I made sure to let them know they could call me "daddy" if they wanted to. Emily had called me it once before and it really made me feel a sense of power in the bedroom.

I had some concerns going into this genital gauntlet. The fear of catching something or having an ill-gotten child was all too real. This was no longer about finding love, this was about loving myself. I knew I had to be honest and open about my intentions from the get-go. My worst fear was that I would accidentally lead someone on like I had been led on. That pain can be really hard to bear and I would wish it on no one. God's honest truth was the only way I could feel good about the process and validity in it's results. I was going to be having casual sex with strangers who could easily say no if I was, in their eyes, "too ugly to fuck". I chose not to send out a picture or include one with my ad. The reason for doing so was that I wanted to know that they were making the decision to have sex with me in person, not just collecting pictures or hoping to find someone better. "Am I the best looking guy you can find?" is a much different question then whether or not I was fuckable. Going into this, I knew not all people were going to be nice. Some were going to be cruel and I knew cruelty all too well.

One of my earliest memories taught me how cruel

people can really be. Strangers do not have to give a single fuck about your life and will prove that given the opportunity. It was a warm summer day back when I was maybe four or five. My mother and father were tending to the garden as my sister and I kicked a ball around in the

yard. My father had the genius idea that instead of taking the time to cut out a large root of a weed, he would simply light it on fire and all would be well. He stood there dousing the poor weed in lighter fluid and throwing matches on it in an attempt to get it to light. Not long after he started disaster struck- the weed was lit but he could not tell that due to the bright sun overhead. He squeezed the bottle of fluid again and fire raced up the stream, exploding the bottle in his hands.

We were terrified. My father was screaming, panicked as he flailed his arm whipping fire around the yard. He was desperately trying to put himself out but was making it so much worse. His arm was ablaze as my mother repeatedly tried to put him out with whatever she could find. My sister and I locked eyes, terrified of what we saw. Our only option was run for help. Sprinting to the back of the yard which led up to an alley, we saw two young ladies passing by and got their attention. We pleaded, "Help us! Help us! Our daddy's on fire!" They walked up, saw the yard and my father aflame, laughed heartily, and walked away. The wounds my father got that day were only skin deep. He ended up making a full recovery. Jesus help me, I wish I could say the same.

Taking the cruelty of society into full account and not wanting to bear any children I knew that every encounter should be with a condom on. I needed to keep myself and all of my future partners safe and I could not put my trust in a complete stranger to hand me a condom. People are sick and might poke holes in it. I also knew that I should pull out before finishing so if and when a condom should fail, I would still not be a father. No money was to be exchanged during this journey. Anyone who needed money to fuck me was not accepting me for who I really was and was out of the running all together. My options on meeting people were low. I was too young to go to a bar or the club. The Internet ended up becoming my stomping grounds. Mind you, this was before the days of swiping left and right. My target audience was the online classifieds. The personal ads would be my salvation.

My knowledge of the human body was limited. Yes, I had had sex, but what did I really know? The biological basics of reproduction are a good start but I did not want to be a low quality partner. I wanted to be remembered, for them to feel things they have never felt before. I didn't need to be the best, I just did not want to be the worst. Books, forums, and even a few magazines gave me the information I needed to fill in the gaps. If you're gonna do something, put your whole heart into it. It took about a month of research before I truly felt confident walking in knowing I had left little to no book knowledge undiscovered that was relative to the task at hand.

The overall concept was simple. I'd find an ad I liked, send them an email, and hope they choose me. Over time I learned roughly nine out of ten ads were people from India trying to steal my email address. The real women were sprinkled in but you had to dig to find them. Some gave you an address on the first email while others would message back and forth for hours, days, or even weeks before making a call as to whether or not you were worthy. For them it was a game. Perhaps just a way for them to get some attention that they were lacking at home. There were plenty of suitors looking to fill their needs and I had to convince a complete stranger to have sex with me over all others. Without ever having met me or seen my image they had to commit to get down with whoever showed up at their door. I had to convince someone to let me not only into their home, but into their body. It is not easily said, let alone done.

To prove you were real was easy enough. Change the subject line and message them something that is not too generic. Only when it was a deal breaker without one would I send a picture. More than likely I have sent the occasional photo to a creepy man pretending to be a woman. No skin off my bones, I hope he enjoys it. Pic collectors were a real thing and if they asked for too many I just stopped responding. Convincing someone you're real is easy, but convincing someone you're safe is much harder. How can you convey over email that you're not a murderer? That you're not a rapist? That you don't have an std that cannot be cured? No one really knows until it's too late. It was a risk we all took and just tried not to think about. For safety, every time I went inside a stranger's house I had two numbers I would text. They were friends who would report me missing if I did not respond at an agreed-upon time. The only lifeline I had if things went south was that the police would know the last place I was, when I was there, and the email address of the person I was talking to.

The time had come, I decided rather then fan through the ads and deal with that end of it I would try posting an ad myself. I was very open and honest, which led me to receive a massive amount of responses. Ninety nine percent of those turned out to be fake. One was real, which made it awfully easy to pick which one to go with. Well, at least you would think that. The description of the woman was very nice and I was excited. The issue lied in that there was also a man. They were a set and solo play was not an option.

I had never even thought about being with a couple before. Even though there was a promise of only heterosexual play, I had reservations. I did not want my first experience posting an ad to end in a sword fight. The idea grew on me, however. It would be a new life experience and definitely an interesting first choice right out of the gate. Nervously, I hopped on my motorcycle and rode toward their place. I only stopped to pick up some condoms and send out my, "hey if you don't hear from me-" texts. I was off, charging headfirst bravely into the unknown. I was hoping for the best but fully aware it could go south in an instant.

Darkness enveloped the area I parked at. It was an unnatural sort of darkness where you can barely make out a face standing ten feet away. As I approached the door, I saw it crack open and the faint outline of a mans face peering from inside. My adrenaline was flowing through me like lava. As I approached the porch the only truly noticeable feature was the dim moonlight reflecting off his glasses. He opened the door to let me inside, it took everything I had not to panic. At least he was wearing pants.

As I stepped through that doorway, not a sound could be heard except my heartbeat thundering in my ears. As the door clicked shut my eyes were flying around the room trying to get a grasp on my surroundings. I saw no woman. No lights were on except one coming from upstairs, a mere glow in the hallway from the bottom. A raspy whisper broke the silence.
"The kids are sleeping so we have to keep quiet. Go upstairs, first door on your right."
A nod was all I could muster as I realized that I had succeeded. If there were kids, there was more than likely a woman waiting for me at the top of the stairs.

Each step brought me closer and closer to my destiny. Each creak so much louder then normal. The man who let me in was not too bad looking, a typical dad body with thinning hair and a well-defined goatee. My hope was that because he had decent looks that the wife was attractive as well. Personally, I got a big rush off the sense of anonymity from the hookups I participated in. It made it like Christmas morning, you had no idea what lied under the wrappings but a strong hope it was something you wanted. As my ascension finished I could see the corner of the bed. There was no turning back, whether this was the path to glory or a trap to take me to the grave, it would all be over soon.

My ears were ringing, my legs shook, and my heart was running a mile a minute as I slowly pressed open the door to see what lay beyond. Thank god, a woman. Wrapped in golden sheets, her smile her only visible defining feature. She was clearly happy at what had arrived as what I was then told was her birthday present. A dozen candles were spread around the room creating an atmosphere of divine fragrance and illumination. My mind went blank as the door clicked shut behind me. The man, wasting no time, walked past me and pulled off the sheets. She blushed as I gazed at her body. Her figure was that of an office secretary, or at least how I'd always pictured one- nice and plump with some decent tits and a very plump ass. Her auburn hair reached her shoulders and her warm brown eyes were framed with think lashes. Not a bad first notch if I do say so myself.

The husband wasted no time in getting the show on the road. He got her on all fours and took the spot behind her before I could even unbuckle my jeans. Within seconds, however, my pants had hit the floor and I approached the bed. She happily accepted me between her lips. Her mouth was so warm it was difficult to hold back. No discussion was had on what was okay and what was not so I contained myself through the intense ordeal. If it was this good up front I could only hope it was as good around back.

Whether it had been two minutes or twenty I could not tell you. Time seemed to stand still as my man meat became well acquainted with her tonsils. The man, tired from his rabbit like thrusting finally withdrew and ordered us to switch spots. It just hit me that he may have left me sloppy seconds. A donut with too much filling. Fuck it, I had gone this far, what did I have to lose? As we rotated I couldn't help but get a look at his equipment. I was bigger, much bigger. Now it all made sense. She needed this, she didn't just want it. Her man, try as he might, was not satisfying her. Someone had to.

As she began to give the husband the same treatment she had given me I quickly slipped on a condom and found my way inside. I went in slow and deep, deeper then he could have ever gone. I felt her sex happily cleave to accommodate me. Her hands firmly grabbed the sheets as I rocked in and out. Her ass fully compressed as I pulled her firmly against me by her hips. She was a bigger girl and the bed was shaking heavily from her rocking. I told her to lay on her back. She happily obliged.

The sucking of her husband resumed and I was now left with a much better angle. I tossed her legs on my shoulders and began to slam into her- each time watching her face scrunch and then go to a smile. As I looked down I could see her clit had swollen to the size of a cashew. I danced a finger lightly around it and she began to moan. For several minutes I did this bringing her closer and closer to orgasm. I wanted her to cum harder then she ever had before. Over the course of my studies on sex I had read about a tactic that claimed to work every time. Who better to try it on?

Gently I withdrew from her and fell to my knees. My fingers slid inside, gently raking her g-spot as I began to suck on her heavily swollen clit. After a few seconds she could not hold back any longer, she could not continue sucking for she was cumming like she never came before. Her thighs locked tightly around my head but I did not slow down. This could go further. She yelped, "Fuck fuck fuck fuck fuck!!!!" as my chin and neck became doused with her juices. I gently eased off the suction and stood up. Mission accomplished, at least for her anyway.

Honestly, I thought it would take longer but after being deprived for so long she was ready to burst. I was just the prick to cause the explosion.

The man stood there confused, not knowing what had happened or why she had never done that for him before. I sensed some jealousy, but the show had to go on. I stood back gently fluffing myself.
"So, where should I finish?" With how quickly she answered I could tell she had thought about this answer quite a bit. "I want you BOTH to finish in my mouth," she said as she lay there on her now soggy part of the mattress. Easy enough, I was pretty worked

up and ready to unload. Her man seemed willing as well.

The dueling commenced. Each man choking his chicken like there was no tomorrow. Maybe sixty seconds had gone by before I saw a tiny spurt hit her face. Kind of sad really on the quantity. Perhaps they had been having fun earlier and his tank was running low. Who knows? All I know is clearly the best was saved for last. As my hand vigorously played the skin flute I felt the pressure building. A lone stream of cum was on her face and it needed reinforcements. My hips bucked as I pumped out every drop I could onto her. Bitch should have had a bowl of cereal waiting for that milk. I did my best to fill her mouth and gently blast off the small streak her man had left. Her tongue was the red carpet I had been waiting for all night long.

With that, I gathered my things and slowly put my tender self back in my clothing. Her husband escorted me to the door. There was no thank you, no offer to return. I guess this was either a one time thing or I had done too well. Either way, I was fully satisfied. My cock was drained and I felt great. I sent my, "hey I'm alive don't worry-" , texts out as I made my way back to my motorcycle. The cool air of the night helped bring me back down to reality. I had just fucked a couple. It was definitely different but also something I would do again, given the opportunity of course. The thought of her hot mouth and the look of elation on her face will forever stick with me. One down, only forty nine more to go.

This next part goes out to the reader directly. Certain things were covered in this chapter that may not be well known in the community and I want to make sure it gets covered. Although female ejaculation was briefly depicted in chapter two, this instance is the first encounter where it was done intentionally. If you were unaware , now you know. Men ejaculate and so do women. The method I covered in this chapter has been the most successful tactic I have employed to achieve female ejaculation in all my years of practice. Over time I have worked to perfect the technique but as a general guideline this is what you should start with. This may not work on all because as we all know, " different strokes for different folks".

Now the way to achieve this very powerful form of orgasm is to stimulate the g-spot. There are other methods and some can finish from the other methods but traditionally direct g-spot stimulation is the way to go. For most, not all but most, women the g-spot is roughly one and a half inches deep located directly behind the pubic bone. You can apply friction, vibration, or pressure to the area to achieve your desired result. This area will become rough to the touch when it is stimulated.

For the woman, in order to squirt, gush, or in proper terms ejaculate you must first understand that you need to relax. Understand that you will feel an urge to pee but this is not pee. What happens as your g-spot is stimulated it swells and draws your fluids into your urethral sponge. These are the fluids that are discharged when you finish and are definitely not urine. The reason you feel the urge to pee is when the sponge swells it puts pressure on your bladder making you feel like you have to urinate. This is one hundred percent normal and a good sign you're doing things right.

    The amazing thing about this process is that unlike a man, a woman has no refractory period. When a man cums he is unable to cum again for a certain amount of time. Intercourse or other stimulation can become painful after he finishes if he were to try and continue. Luckily for women this biological process does not occur and you can squirt over and over again. I personally recommend waiting a minute or two so its more like a roller coaster instead of a never ending drag race, but to each his own. All women can squirt. The only thing preventing them is their own mind (barring no medical abnormalities of course). If you learn only one thing from this book, take this last section and fucking run with it. A large portion of my notches are from teaching women to squirt. It truly is the most fun you can have with your partner behind closed doors.

CHAPTER FOUR

A single mom with a single need

    Although it may have been a cast off into some pretty choppy waters, my voyage had begun. The ice was broken and my belt had achieved it's first notch. The skills I had read about seemed to get the job done in the real world and were not just some made-up fantasy. It is difficult for me to try and comprehend the relationship dynamic that brought me into their bedroom that night. Why exactly was I, of all people, there? My silver tongue spoke highly of my abilities through email and when the time came it had not left them wanting. So, although I cannot take pride in knowing that my first notch was with a single female I can, however take pride in knowing that I was able to give her something she needed. I gave her something that, try as he might, her husband just could not deliver.

    There seemed to be no way to guarantee a steady flow of partners. For some reason or another people came and left as they saw fit, filling whatever needs they had and departing. If I could have kept a steady pace, my task would have been done in a just one year instead of seven. Several failed attempts in a row left me down, but not out. The drive to breed is alive and well in me and no amount of failure can put out that flame. To say my standards were low could be seen as an understatement to some. To others, I just seemed humble. I cared little of one's appearance, abilities, or social status. My only concern was that they truly wanted to have sex with me, sounded honest, and had a pulse. For my second notch the bar was set at, "a single individual with a vagina".

    Scammers, perverts, and my competition relentlessly flooded my inbox with false hope, degradation, and bitterness. The amount of times I was contacted by men was insane. Every Tom, Dick, and Harry wanted a piece of me and sounded super desperate. I tried to be polite but more often than not a simple 'no' would not get through to them. Somehow it became my duty to defend my position on why I, a single male who assumed he was heterosexual, did not want a blowjob from a man. I was offered money and drugs but their offers fell on deaf ears. The highest offer I got was $300 to receive oral sex from a man and at the time I almost said yes. A week's worth of wages to lay back and get head sounded pretty sweet. Deep down I felt it was wrong so I passed on the offer.

    It was my third week of attempting to find someone when I finally got in touch with notch number two. The hunt began at roughly eight but I did not hear from her until three in the morning. It was the Hail Mary booty call in the eleventh hour. She claimed to be recently divorced and looking to gain some new experiences before going back into the dating world. My offer to give her the dicking down of her life to help her get over her husband intrigued her greatly. She set the time and the place. Five in the morning is when I arrived at her front door with a lone condom in hand. She told me right from the start I had to be out of the house by six, no later. I agreed, as the night had worn on me. Although I was excited and highly aroused at the prospect of meeting her my body grew weary from being up all night.

As the door opened I was hit by a strong odor of marijuana. I had always been drug free and was not about to change that now. She graciously invited me into her home and led me to her bedroom. This was nothing like the first notch in the way of social interaction. She seemed friendly and was very willing to talk. Whether it was because she was nervous, lonely, or high as a kite I have no idea. She told me how she worked at the hospital just a few minutes away and had just gotten home from work. Her light blue scrubs definitely kept my attention. Sitting against her curves even fully dressed I could tell I was in for a treat. She was a busty Latina with an ass so fat you could put a phone book in between the cheeks. She was larger than a D cup, more breast than I knew what to do with. She was bbw and very proud of it.

I checked my phone to make sure my safety texts had sent and as I looked back up I saw her for the first time without her scrubs on. Although she was on the larger side she had no stretch marks. I gazed upon her figure as she walked towards me. My eyes bounced back and forth between her large breasts and the small bush she had going on downstairs. No sooner had I put my phone back in my pocket did she push me back on the bed and pull down my fly. I had not expected her to want to take the bull by the horns like that. She was a cougar in every sense of the word. She was a carnivore, lusting for that meat.

Her hands were all over me. She stroked me up and down and played with my balls. It was very relaxing to have someone so gentle handling you down there. Soon she began to lick and kiss my shaft as she still used both hands on me. The sensations were intense and my wiggling and moaning were getting her even more wound up. As much as I wanted to keep going and coat the back of her throat right then and there I was aware that she wanted me inside her before the hour was up. I saw an alarm clock beside the bed and somehow it was already five thirty. We only had a half hour to go and I had not even touched her yet.

I leaned forward to play with her breasts. Not to pull her away from her oral activities, but to show her that she would be getting some attention as well. Her somewhat massive areolas were my targets and she did not seem to mind that one bit. She relinquished me from her mouth and stood up. I slid my jeans to the ground and she started going down.
"Woah woah woah!" I said, showing her the condom in my hand.
She apologized profusely, afraid that she had

scared me off. She explained that she was so used to riding her husband and that they never used condoms. Everything was okay, she had not touched it yet. Good thing, too, because as I rolled on the condom a drop of pre-cum was already trying to escape.

As she slid on down right to the base of my cock I was in heaven. Her love tunnel happily wrapped around me as she rocked forward and backwards. Her ass was all I could really see and take hold of as we played the mattress symphony. The bed was not the sturdiest one ever built. It was constructed to handle either my weight, or hers, not both at once. The rocking was intense as the springs and frame screeched and begged for mercy. The dwarven craftsman who made it should be very proud.

She could literally take me no deeper and with each firm bounce down I swear I could feel the pressure of her cervix pushing back on me. I never wanted the feeling to end but I turned once again to the clock. It was five fifty five in the morning and only five minutes remained in our time together.

I let her know the hour was almost up. She stopped riding me and looked at the clock. She looked more scared then happy. She turned to me, eyes bloodshot but open as wide as they could and said, "What is the fastest way to make you cum?"

I thought she would never ask. "Ride me like you stole me- I'll finish in no time."

She gave her all she fucking had, captain, thundering up and down like she was a jockey in a horse race. The bed somehow defied modern science and survived despite it's questionable craftsmanship. My head pounded her cervix, the pressure of her weight, and the feeling of her juicy meat curtains ever so lightly threw me over the edge. I held her tight as I felt myself explode inside her. She came as well and her cunt squeezed my cock like it was making a fresh glass of orange juice. Only a thin piece of latex separated that load from her inviting fuckhole. Had it not held it would have been clean up in aisle three. You would have needed a mop and a wet floor sign for sure. I turned one last time to the clock. Six a.m. on the dot, perfect timing. I took a deep sigh of relief as she hopped off. "Finished just in time, huh?" I said with a smile.

She did not return the smile in kind.

"That clock's five minutes slow, I need you to get the fuck out of here, now!" she said firmly trying to get re-dressed. She was getting her scrubs back on as I tried pulling up my pants with my member still swelled. Never dressed so fast in my life, to be honest, but in her eyes I was still not moving quick enough. She guided me to the door with force and shut it behind me. What the fuck was her problem? Maybe she was just super OCD about the time for no real reason? I took the t-shirt which had been haphazardly tossed over my shoulder and put it on as I walked back to where I had parked my motorcycle. She roared to life like always and I was letting her warm up for a bit before I rode home. I sent my usual, "hey I'm alive don't worry" texts, and put my bike into gear.

Before taking off, I always check my mirrors. The coast was clear in the left but on the right there was a man. He was walking up to the house I had just left. I popped it back into neutral, carefully watching what happened next. Was he another suitor she had lined up? Was I not the first person she had over that night? What exactly was going on? Then I noticed him reach into his pocket and pull out a set of keys. This was her husband, or ex-husband, or boyfriend, or- whoever the fuck it was I did

not want to stick around and find out. As he went inside I gently putted away. The air stung my eyes, which were irritated from all the smoke they had been exposed to.

Everything she said could have been a lie. From where she worked to her relationship status. Although I always hoped for honesty I knew some people out there were going to use me to cheat on their spouse. If that was true karma would come knocking in no time. At the very least I had my notch and nothing could take that away from me. Whats done is done and nothing could change that. Would that man ever know? I know he didn't see me leave the house or he would have been watching me. Was she able to get the bed back in order before I left? Would he notice the sex was different after she had spent the past hour pleasing me? My guess is he probably never knew I was in the house unless- and this is a big unless- he found the massively overloaded condom I left on the floor on his side of the bed.

CHAPTER FIVE

Anything for a friend

My confidence was soaring with my newly discovered talents. Not only was I able to convince a complete stranger to hop into bed with me but I was also able to make them feel things they had never felt before. The quest for sexual knowledge I had undertaken continued to pay dividends each time I hit the sheets. Amongst a select group of friends I had managed not to push away, the topic of sex eventually came up and I could not help but brag about my recent successes. Others lacked the confidence to do what I did. Leave home in the middle of the night not knowing who exactly you were going to meet. If a friend asks for help- you help them in any way you can, always.

Telling someone how to ride a bike and pushing them while they pedal are two different ways to get the job done. You can try the first, but more than likely issues will arise. They can fail and, ultimately, lose confidence. The methods I used to obtain my notches were explained to a friend who needed the most help.

He had graduated a year ahead of me in high school yet still remained a virgin, much to his chagrin. His name was Todd and he had a similar build to myself but stood only five eight. Todd tried over and over but could not seem to reel in a catch. It was time for me to jump in the dinghy and help with the net.

Thankfully, I was not alone in this journey of finding moisture for good ole cactus cock. Greg, a mutual friend of ours, both did not want to stand idly by and watch us struggle alone. We became a testosterone task force to be reckoned with. A testicular triumvirate the likes of which the world had never seen. For us the objective was clear, we were looking to find a woman who was looking to be completely dominated. The three of us could each get a hole if we wanted, no need to double dip. The planning was easy, finding a willing participant was not.

We remained open to suggestions in the ad. Open to a train like system or all at once. Having been on the the online classifieds over a year this was far from my first rodeo. No one in the group had done anything like this before so in the heat of the moment all bets were off. The only rule was no guy on guy contact, not even eyes. After a few weeks of trying we find our first hit.

It was August 11th, 2012 when we finally struck oil, or so we thought. A late Saturday evening drive roughly an hour away to a secluded side street in Todd's mothers minivan. Not the cleanest or most presentable vehicle but it had the space we needed if it came to having car fun. This was the longest I had ever driven to get some action, but it felt worth it for Todd. We sat in that van close to twenty minutes before our guest of honor made her debut. Her headlights blinded us as she pulled up to ten feet directly in front of us in this narrow street.

We may have been a little nervous, but we were all willing. Determined to do whatever it took to get Todd over the hump. I cannot say this is quite "taking one for the team", as I was also going to be benefiting from the exchange. We had the rubbers and we had the will, she alone stood as the decider of whether this went down tonight. A quick overlooking judgment was all she had time for. There was no time for a cup of coffee and getting to know each other - no, this was gonna have to be a quick decision of "yes, I do" want to have sex with this group of young men or "no, I do not" want to do so.

She shut off her car and walked straight at us. The only sound breaking the silence of the night was the clicking of her heels. She was tall, close to six foot one if I had to guess and the heels added even more to her stature. She had a silver necklace that sparkled from the streetlight. A dark blue full length dress, the same shade as the heels, fitted her snugly. She was a cougar if I have ever seen one. Busty, thin, and a beautiful face you could barely make out through her long blond hair. She would make a fine first for Todd.

She leaned in the window and gave us all a once

over. She seemed pleased with what she saw, or so we thought. A thirty second shaky conversation and the conditions were set. We were to follow her back to her place, have our fun, and be out by midnight. It had just turned ten and we were excited at the prospects of having two full hours with her. This would allow Todd to have his first time by himself, then, once he had run himself ragged Greg and I would come in to finish the job. Easy peasy lemon squeazy.

Casually she strolled back to her car, her ass shook intentionally, giving us a good show as we casually walked back to the car.

She didn't waste a second, though, between getting in her car and making her great escape. She flew past us at a speed the van could not reach on this short side street. By the time we had pulled our three point turn she was gone, long gone. We floored it to the end of the block to see if maybe it had been some kind of joke. Maybe she lived right around the corner? Alas, her small car was nowhere to be seen. Defeated, we drove to a nearby gas station to try and contact her. After a half hour she messaged back finally letting us know she had chickened out. She loved the idea of being with us, but she was too scared to actually go through with it. Try as I might, my silver tongue could not lure her in.

After that massive failure we were definitely disheartened. The crew was in too low spirits to try the following week. The project was almost scrapped as doubt set in. I spent the whole week trying to rally the men and convince them the venture was not all for naught. We got to planning and I tried again the next Saturday night. No one had expected to succeed after the difficulty in attaining our first interest. To our surprise we got a hit. August 25th, 2012 was the day we found her.

From the sound of the email she was our holy grail. Five foot tall, 44DD chest, and (best of all) just eighteen years old. The email had come in around ten and by eleven we were all sitting outside her place waiting for her to appear. I was the wheelman that night so Greg could ride shotgun, leaving Todd to man the backseat. Hopefully the ride to the hotel I had picked out would give him enough time to be well acquainted with our new-found cum dumpster.

She lived in the suburbs so we were not graced with the benefit of streetlights. A dark figure matching the description came through the door she had described as hers in the email. We rolled up and tossed her in, making as quick a getaway from her parents place as we could without drawing suspicion. I pulled away ever so gently pressing on the accelerator. She was real, not only real but matched her description. She was five foot, had a massive chest, and was the age she claimed to be. A detail had been left out of her synopsis. She was black.

I do not know why I assumed she would be white. The topic of race had never come up and it had specifically said in the ad that all races were equally welcome. Guess it just came as a shock more then anything. Her race mattered not what mattered were the events about to take place. This barely legal girl was riding with us, headed at highway speed to the hotel I had chosen, fully intent on hours of fun. Everyone, including Todd, was wearing a smile.

Things never seem to go quite as planned in these casual encounters we have. We had the manpower, the girl, even the rubbers. What we did not have was the consent of the hotel. As it turns out, at least at the time, in the state of Pennsylvania you must be a minimum of twenty five years of age to rent a hotel. Even though I had a credit card, and was consenting to put down any deposit they deemed necessary, still I was denied. Cheer turned to sorrow as I broke the news. No one really wanted to have this event at their place for obvious reasons. Even if we made it past the family, the sound would give us away. Plan B was a go.

Plan B was not ideal, nor nearly as pleasurable. It involved us parking at a local shopping center, marching across the street into a park, and if all went as planned have crazy sex behind the little league concession stand. The woods were a good cover around the stand to muffle the sound. The large landscaping rocks made a perfect seat or table to lay on. It did not need to be perfect, just enough to get the job done.

She was still a very willing participant in all this. Just as eager as us to get to the action. The concept of playing out in public seemed to wet her whistle just as much as it did mine. The facts remained the same though, we still had to get her back in a reasonable time so her family would not notice her absence. We drove to the shopping center and parked as inconspicuously as possible. We were one of three cars in the lot, but who cared. We made our way across the street and up the hill towards the site of sin. I fumbled in the dark, head on a swivel making sure we were not being watched or followed. As I looked back I could see the burger joint where I was offered oral sex for a cheeseburger. A sense of leaving the past in the past and starting fresh fell upon me. I was surely not the man I was back then, but that says nothing of what I was that night.

The woods filled with a literal army of cicadas aided us in not drawing any undue attention. Any sounds or screams we made would drown out long before reaching the road. We had arrived, the debauchery nary a moment away. The moonlight let me see our sexual sacrifice in a whole new way. Her thighs had just enough meat on them to make you want to use them as earmuffs. Her ass was in a league all its own. A cute smile across her beautiful face made you melt and ooze instantly. She was wearing a plaid green mini skirt just long enough to cover her panties. There was no reason to delay, Todd had waited long enough.

It was agreed in the car that because it was his first time, Todd should get first crack at it while we kept watch. Greg and I left them to their own devices while we went around to stand guard. We were both ready to bounce if given the signal. While we were standing there blowing the breeze I could not help but notice that Greg was just as excited as I was. His jeans straining to contain a piece of man meat about an inch longer then my own by the look of it.

Ten minutes or so had gone by and I was becoming restless. The signal was not given, nor were there any sounds of life back there. I hadn't even taken two steps to go check on them when they both appeared.
" So how was it buddy?" I asked hoping they had just been real quiet. I was not as lucky as I had hoped. Todd, in his nervousness, had his member pulling a scared turtle. Not willing to end the evening so early I sent back Greg and had a heart to heart with Todd on what was happening. He claimed to never have an issue before so I had hope that he could work past it. I told him to do some deep breathing and there was no pressure for him to perform. He casually threw on some porn while smoking a cigarette, trying to get his little man to attention. I left him to it, eager to see how Greg was making out.

When I rounded the corner she was on her knees happily bobbing up and down on him as he lay sprawled out on one of the many rocks. His eyes closed and hands behind his head just enjoying the attention. I stood there watching in the darkness. The sound of her gagging on his girth a symphony in the night. I became incredibly aroused, staring intently at her underwear, fully exposed from her position. They were neon pink and firmly wedged in a fine camel toe. My heart was racing and my mouth became dry.

Hypnotized by what lay before me I felt myself getting close to finishing from the sight alone. A rhythmic pulsing down below begging to bust out. I damn near came when I felt a hand touch my shoulder.

Thank god it was Todd. He had snapped me out of my trance to tell me that all hope was lost and to just try and forget about him and have my fun. For some reason I could not let him give up until every stone was turned over. Begrudgingly I retreated from the front line to try and help Todd one last time. Willing to do anything to help a friend we tried one last, albeit quit stupid looking back on it, hail mary attempt at achieving erection. If this did not work I was resigned to defeat, unable to help him. I ordered him to lay on his back with his feet in the air. I would hold his legs while he went to town on himself, praying that blood supply was the only issue. It was our only chance and we took it. Quite awkward holding a guys legs in the air while he tugs himself. Cannot imagine it any better being the guy doing the tugging. After a few minutes we abandoned the idea. It was worth a try wasn't it?

I rounded the corner to find Greg balls deep inside her. She was seated on his massive rod, moaning as her tits swung with every bounce. Her shaved cunt clearly exposed to the world as her skirt had made itself scarce. I ordered her to flip and she happily obliged. Sliding off Greg's condom and returned him to her mouth. I knew with how worked up I was if I had started in her mouth I would have never left it. I wanted that glistening little fuckhole that drew your eye in the moonlight. Cleanly shaved with skin as smooth as silk.

I approached her, dawning my armor ready to charge into battle. As the tip went in I could feel her pussy try and pull me in, I let it. That bear trap of a meat pocket locked so firmly around my member I could feel her pulse. I thrust in and out, incredibly cautious as to not spill the precious cargo. I could tell Greg was about to finish. He grabbed a hand full of her hair and forced her down firmly against him. No complaints, she was happy to suck out every drop he could muster. She withdrew, as did I. Greg was down for the count, she was all mine.

Sliding off the condom got her attention. Her mouth was the only target that made sense. A moment longer and I was going to bust inside her even with a condom on. She licked her lips as I approached her, ready to unload an avalanche down inside her. She hummed as she sucked, sending shivers down the shaft all the way to the balls. This was clearly not her first time. I wanted to coat her throat badly , but at the same time I wanted more. She was like no pussy I had ever felt. I wanted, no, I *needed* to feel it raw. As I withdrew I told her to sit up on a rock. She nodded and quickly did what she was told. We were inches apart as I told her, not asked, " I'm going in raw but I promise I won't cum inside." She nodded, accepting her fate.

Her sex radiated heat like a furnace as she scooted forward just enough to give me the angle I needed. This girl redefined hot-to-trot. As I entered her I was overcome with joy. The heat of her breath on my neck as I speared her deep. The sounds of her as I rocked in and out gently bouncing off her sore cervix at every thrust. She was tired and ready to finish. Her sex was quickly becoming sore. Her cunt beaten within an inch of its life by Greg, left me with only the finishing blows. The urge to finish inside was high, was I not a man of my word I would have put a baby in her right then and there. Lucky for her I am an honest man and withdrew just in time to force her down and explode all over her. The chest, the hair, the face, and finally the sweet swirling tongue consumed me. Draining every last swimmer I had down her throat.

She was drenched. I had never cum so hard in my life. She was impressed, the guys were impressed, I was impressed. We cleaned her up as best we could with a t shirt and headed for the car. A much slower walk going out then it had been going in. We actually caught a break having Todd be too nervous. Had he been a participant we probably would have had to carry her out.

To say that was a baptism by fire would not be fair, more like napalm. Throwing him in that situation was not what was best for him, it is what was best for me. I tried to control my friends by turning them into men. Turns out you just cannot do that. Todd and I have lost contact with one another. We had taken a few years off, tried reconnecting but it did not pan out. We were just too different to be friends. As for Greg, last I heard he was still living with his mom, no job or girlfriend.

What happened to the woman who made that night a reality? As we dropped her off she had a smile ear to ear. About a month later she was happy when we stopped just hooking up and decided to go on our first date. A couple months go by and she's ecstatic when I pop the question. Seven years to the day after that night we both had tears in our eyes, tears of joy, as we were finally made husband and wife.

CHAPTER SIX
Am I sure I wanna do this?

Fall was rapidly approaching and my summer of sexual exploration had come to an end. This new way of life was chock-full of risks as well as rewards. My life was now at a crossroads. Over the past month I had continued to see the girl that we had so magnificently defiled at the park. No longer could I continue to put my friends at risk when they could not perform in the heat of the moment. From now on it was all about number one.

Was I truly happy with my newfound lover, or was it just some self-sculpted reality giving me perceived happiness? Was any woman my own age that I took to bed magically a goddess like her? The only way I would know for sure was if I were to lay with another and not feel the same feelings. For this attempt, I tried my luck with online dating sites. What a crock.

For starters, the majority of the profiles on the dating sites I used were not active. I, being the cheap son of a bitch that I am, would not pay for dating sites.

Why I was unwilling to part with even a few dollars was beyond me. Being raised in a frugal household where pennies must be pinched so mommy and daddy can get their fix kind of rubs off on you. Hell, my father is so thrifty he even tried to sell an empty (but definitely used) urn at a yard sale. There were tiny flecks of grandpa still inside. Wish that part was a joke but sadly it is not.

After messaging hundreds of profiles I finally found someone willing to spend the day with me. Guaranteed sex with no expectation of any future contact were the agreed upon terms. A mere forty five minute drive stood between me and my answer. Upon arrival it quickly became evident she had used every trick in the book to try and mask her flaws. In the real world she was still relatively attractive, maybe more than I deserved, but far from the girl who I thought I was meeting. Her mole, roughly the size of a dime, must have just popped up overnight. The thing that caught me off guard the most, however, were the hearing aids.

Do not misinterpret being caught off guard as being intolerant. I was more than willing to date a woman hard of hearing, even kind of excited by the idea. To not put
that in her profile seemed... dishonest. It wasn't the best launching place for any relationship. I thought less of her right from the start, be proud of what you are- it makes you unique.

The drive back to my place would be considered

by most less then romantic- highway driving with all the windows down to stay cool. She was unable to hear practically anything I tried to say. The wind noise easily overwhelmed the hearing aids leaving us to cruise in silence after several failed attempts at even the most basic communication. As we arrived at my place I realized that I had never before brought a girl home. I had no idea how my parents would react as I casually walked a girl through the living room and took her upstairs. I had not thought to mention her at any time before our arrival.

    Luckily, they let us pass. There were looks of confusion and definite concern, but no objection. Just a casual, "hey we'll be upstairs," was all I could think to say as we snuck by. What was I supposed to say? "Hey mom, hey dad, this is a random skank I picked up online. I know this may sound crazy but I am going to have sex with her for a specific reason. I need to make sure I am actually in love with a different woman of questionable repute I have been involved with recently." In that instance I decided less was more.

    We made our way to my room, which just happened to be the attic. As we climbed I couldn't help but play with her ass. A sneak peek of what I was hoping to get at the top of the stairs. She had not dressed the part of a slut by any means. Sweatpants and a rock band t shirt were all my imagination had to work with. Still, even though she had thick curves she wore them well. I was, and would still be to this day, physically attracted to her. At this junction that was the only prerequisite to coitus.

Things began to get hot and heavy once we jumped into bed and it was obvious this was not something she did often. Her inexperience was not too much of a obstacle to overcome but her lack of skills and unwillingness to try were definitely burdensome. She wanted not to have a quick fuck, but to make love- an intimate session of kisses and a warm embrace. My intentions were clear as crystal from the very beginning. I wanted no commitment. To deny her what she wanted seemed rude so I gave in. I smothered her with passionate kisses, adding what little romance I was capable of in the heat of the moment. She was catching feelings before I even got inside her.

My goal remained the same regardless of her clear misunderstanding of what I was after. I began to explore, my hands ravaging her figure. Her bush had never seen a gardener. She wanted me, more then I wanted her. She told me to lay back as she began to strip. As her clothes hit the floor my cock filled with blood. I quickly lost my pants, ready to receive what she had to offer. If only I knew the horror that was about to unfold I would have stopped right then and there. Quickly I ripped open a condom from my bedside table and slid it on. There I lay, a very aroused twenty year old waiting for a plus sized girl to hop on and ride me. She wasted no time mounting me. Forcing me inside, her juices thick and slimy. The smell of her musk intense and unpleasant.

This was not the first time I had been scarred by sex, nor would it be the last. Prior to hopping on she had popped her hearing aids out. Her eyes were closed and she was basically riding me like the world around her did not exist. I kept popping out, each time being forced back in on the violent down stroke. I feared her snapping me like a twig. It felt good, don't get me wrong, just not good enough for the risk. A minute of so later she stopped riding. Stopping at the bottom and shivering. She had cum, at least one of us could cum from that. She laid beside me, kissing me on the chest and told me she loved me. I was not about to return the words.

She looked at me, trying to think of a way to win me over. Her head slid down to my still erect cock. Carefully she slid the condom off and began to lick and suck me. Once again I was in fear as her inexperience put my genitals in jeopardy. The rhythm was fine, so was the moisture. I was happy she was removing that musky pussy stink off me but unhappy that I was becoming more and more acquainted with her molars. Every third or fourth dip down meant a little brush with a bicuspid or a collision with a canine. In the attempt to put another notch in my belt, this notch was attempting to put a notch in me. I leaned up, whispering for her to stop but she could not hear me without the hearing aids. I did not want to spook her, heaven forbid she panic and chomp down. I sat in silence, trying not to panic, trying not to cry.

Several minutes passed. No closer was I to cumming than when this whole thing started. I was hard as steel but without a good hole to stick it in I was dead in the water. She stopped, holding me with both hands and squeezed the life out of my little buddy. I was just about to tell her off, tell her to fuck off back to whence she came. That didn't happen. She stared me down, gave me a big set of puppy dog eyes and said, "I want you to fuck my ass."

That line redeemed her. Something I had never done, but always wanted to try. I nodded and she got on all fours, presenting her brown eyed whisperer to the world. At least it smelled better then the front.

I readied myself, using what little lube I had to make things go as smooth as glass. I only had that one condom she had torn off, I needed to nut, I was going in raw. With one firm push I slid all the way in, her tight little asshole pulling me all the way. It was in no way like fucking a pussy, I could feel nothing at the tip. The bottom inch of my cock felt like a hand job from a gorilla. Her anus held me tight as I rocked in and out, edging myself. Getting near my breaking point and backing off, I wanted this to be a huge load, to go off like a hydrant all over her.

The noises she made were the combination of pleasure and a baby otter being beaten in a burlap sack. She could not hear herself, or if she could, had no idea what noises sound sexy to a man as he rails your tailpipe. I was on the brink of orgasm, my achy cock exhausted from the anal assault. Thirty more seconds and I was going to pull out, letting this cum volcano erupt all over her back. She began to rock, her moans growing louder, a lone phrase escaped her lips, "Cum inside my ass, daddy."

The intensity was too much, her wish became my command. My fingers dug deep in her sides as I released inside of her. Torrents of cum flooded her insides. A sigh of relief escaped me. Even after cumming inside, I felt nothing for this girl. No love, no deeper connection, just a mild combination of fear and arousal. I felt forced out of there by the pressure I had created. You know what they say- a blowjob will make your day- but anal will make your hole weak. Slowly but surely the river started to flow out. She maintained her pose on all fours, letting the cum run out onto my mattress. If only I had owned a sheet it would not have been so bad.

I had erroneously assumed that my ejaculation would be my salvation when it ended up being my damnation. I reached over and grabbed my shirt to wipe myself off. The shirt was bright red and had an eagle on it. No sooner had I finished wiping myself off that I saw it happen right before my very eyes. Perhaps she did not even feel it because of the rectal road rash. She was blissfully unaware that the river of cum had carried a log down stream. It had fallen out and made a slight splash sending the puddle of runny cum out in all directions. I was fucking mortified.

Freedom isn't free, and neither was that shirt. Before she even knew her blunder I leaned forward and cleaned up my mess, as well as hers. Not one drop had come anywhere near her pussy so I knew I would avoid being a father for a little while longer. This was not a woman I wanted to reproduce with, she meant nothing. My love truly lied with another. My soulmate, the girl from the park, was truly *the one*. I wanted her to have my babies, not this random dating site trash.

This lesson came at a price. I had lost a shirt, my pride, and quite possibly a mattress. If there was ever an event that occurred to end a date faster then I did that day I would love to know about it. Maybe it is just me but once you poop on my bed I really want you out of my fucking house. A quick pit stop at the shitter (the bathroom, not my fucking bed) to scrub myself clean and we were gone. I felt dirty on the outside and on the inside. To her, the day had gone perfect and we were madly in love. On my side, if I ever saw her again it would be too soon.

I drove her home, the entire ride she talked about our future together. Her mouth never seemed to close. Excited at what we had done, optimistic about our new life together. I told her more then once that I was not looking for a relationship but she would not for the love of god take no for an answer. We arrived at last back at her place. Finally this nightmare could be over. She hopped out smelling of sex, hair disheveled like she was out all night partying.
"I had a great time, I hope you enjoy the rest of your day!" I said, trying to let her down easy.
She leaned in the window, "Aren't you coming in to meet my parents?" She just didn't get it.
"Let me just find a place to park quick," I said, eagerly awaiting her head to exit my car. As soon as she was out, I was gone. My little sedan's tires chirped as I put the force of god on that pedal, determined to

never see, hear, or smell her again.

CHAPTER SEVEN
The ogre in disguise

    Having barely escaped the shitting seductress by my skin on her teeth, I need to reevaluate my priorities. The mattress had to be tossed and a new, upgraded version took its place. This was the first new mattress I had ever gotten. Everything I had received before was the worn out hand me down, or the mattress from so-and-so who just happened to pass away. It was bouncy, not sagged and beaten down from years of service. Its fabric wore not the stains of valor.

    The concept of ending up with a girlfriend through this whole affair truly seemed counter productive. Should I abandon my gauntlet run of manhood so early? The goal was fifty, I was only at ten. Long hours of discussion and mediation were had between Monica and I. Although we both had feelings for one another we both wanted to continue to have sex with other people. A tricky conundrum to say the least. How do you tell someone, " hey once I fuck like forty more people you and I should really settle down and be with one another." Sounds kind of silly doesn't it? We mutually agreed to have an open relationship, quite possibly the greatest decision we ever made.

Imagine for a moment a relationship free of jealousy. Infidelity was no longer something that drew you to anger. Of course there were ground rules- no family, no coworkers, etc. As a whole this system worked for us. Following a long discussion we came to discover that neither of us knew a single couple who had a happy monogamous relationship. None ever seemed to last, and if they did the happiness just was not there.

My father and mother stayed married until her passing in late twenty eighteen. My entire childhood was ripe with accusations of my father cheating , which, he was in fact doing to the best of my knowledge. Regardless of the amount of evidence he left behind as long as he was not caught in the act, he would defend his innocence to the death. She only caught him once, but once is enough. He ended up getting himself caught once by me as well. He was at his local watering hole, had been for several hours. This dumb son of a bitch calls for a ride and *then* proceeds to take the bar whore into the stall to have fun. Why on gods earth would he just not have his fun and then call for a ride after? I show up and he is nowhere to be found. No one in the bar seems to know where he is , so I check the bathroom. As I approach the door a blond woman in a yellow sun dress walks out of the mens room. Blushing heavily, too embarrassed to make eye contact. I push open the door to find my father fumbling with his belt, too drunk to even realize he had been caught. That was the standard of marriage I had to beat.

Our relationship was going quite well. No arguments, just love. We decided we had more then enough energy to share another woman. Monica desperately wanted to make me happy, little did she know her just being with me made me the happiest man alive. The quest to find a unicorn was an arduous one indeed. There is a reason they are called unicorns, they are really, really rare. Most women do not want to be shared by a couple. They either want a man, or a woman, not both. For weeks the only responses we got were from women well into their forties. Not our cup of tea. Monica had been with women before, just a few, but knew what she was doing. We were a pussy and penis powerhouse waiting for our shot to blow the mind of any woman our age willing to take a chance on us.

The concept of adding another to the bedroom always has its risks. Jealousy can spring up if you give it the chance. Each time you engage in a three way there are certain things you need to understand. Although you are very excited to make the third wheel happy, this is not just about them. Your attention should be equally divided amongst them and your original partner. To give preferential treatment is only a disaster waiting to happen. Avoid flattery, this is your foe and can spark conflict. Make sure each partner is fully satisfied before ending the event. Leaving one wanting will ensure it never happens again.

We found plenty of couples who wanted to join us, all were a lie. We knew going into the conversation that they were a lie. Every time a couple messaged us they would want pictures which we sent to hopefully provide enough incentive to get them into bed with us. They would return with pictures of their own, a time and date would be set, everything would be all hunky dory until magically, like fucking clockwork, they would change their mind. Well I should not say they, I can guarantee you that nine out of ten couples out there are just a single guy pretending to be a couple. Usually the morning of the event would be when we would get the email, text, or dm. " Hey its ___, so it turns out blank is on her period/ changed her mind/ having second thoughts etc."

This was not the frustrating part about it. EVERY FUCKING TIME the man would continue, "If you guys are still horny I can come over and have some fun! Maybe we can all have fun next week lol." If you are that guy, and I hope at least one of you reading this is, please stop. I cannot put into words how much I want you to go fuck yourself.

Close to a month had gone by before we finally got a legitimate response. The profile picture had us all hot and bothered. She was the most adorable little Asian girl you ever laid eyes on. Soft features and eggshell skin. We had both heard good things about them in bed, rumor was they were tight and I was interested in finding out how much so. We set up a time for the next day. That night I could hardly sleep as I thought about all the fun which was to come. This was my first time with two girls and I did not want to disappoint. A light and a dark, the ying and yang of arousal.

That afternoon we got the message saying she was on her way. Like a child I was staring out the window, looking for Santa's sleigh. There was a large open parking lot right across the street, I told her to park there and message when she arrived. Today I *was* Santa, ready to bring joy. I wanted her to sit on my lap and tell senpai she was naughty. I wanted tears of joy as I stuffed her stocking, and come hell or high water I was intent on emptying my sack down her chimney.

At last, a car matching the description rolled into the lot. It was her dad's truck, an old brown pickup less a tailgate. Our phone dings, it really is her. We tell her to come on over , we are waiting. I leave Monica upstairs and head down to the living room. Like a little puppy I waited by the door. Luckily we are the only ones home or my obvious erection would more then likely draw suspicion and an awkward stare. A knock at the door, this was it. I flung it open to see our guest. It took a few seconds to process what I was seeing, damn those camera tricks.

She was cute and adorable, just a lot taller then we had imagined. I stand six two and she was looking me in the eye. She was dressed as a tomboy, torn up blue jeans with a worn out camo army jacket up top. I invited her in, still excited to meet her, just caught highly off guard. Once inside I got to give her a full once over. She was thick, but not fat. She had basically no ass and her bra size would make a parent happy if it was on a report card. She was there and she was willing, that's all that mattered. Our unicorn had arrived and I was still determined to enjoy every last second of her company. With a firm slap on what she called her ass, we were off to the bedroom.

The climb to my room offered not much of a view, but it did offer a minute to think. I prayed that Monica would be accepting of the newly discovered form of our guest. Luckily she had made herself comfortable and was waiting for her at the top, sprawled out on the bed offering a nice show. Monica was nude and began to finger herself, leaving our guest to stare at her beauty. I quickly got behind her and started to rub up and down her sides. Slowly I began to unbutton her clothes and placed them on the floor. Under all that fabric she was divine. Porcelain skin with the smallest black bush. She was the china shop, and I was the bull.

I guided our guest down to the mattress, laying her beside Monica. The two began to kiss, quite the sight to behold. Their hands wandered over each others breasts as I took to appeasing organs farther south. One hand on each, enough to go around. Soft moans escaped them as my fingers wandered up and down their slits. Their warm goodness ran up my fingers as I guided each stroke with expert precision. My attention turned to their clits. Both swollen, both yearning to take their master over the threshold. Who would cum first?

The teasing evolved to a firm swirl around their love buttons. My speed increased as they got wetter and wetter. Their light kissing had evolved into heavy frenching. My cock jumped at every moan, eager to get in on the action. Our guest finished first, a few seconds later Monica did as well. They both looked at me, legs swill squirming from excitement. We all knew what it meant, time to switch places.

I laid in the warm spot the two had created as both of them descended upon me like vultures. For me, this was just fun, but for them it felt like a competition. Both of them went at me like rabid dogs. Their hands and tongues desperate for cock. Sure they wanted to share me, switching off every thirty seconds, but they both wanted to be the one to make me finish. Their tongues swirled around me like an all day sucker. I was about to blow, but who should get the honor? Quickly I told both of them to suck me at the same time. Each girl gently rolled a ball in their hand as their tongues fought to the death around my shaft. As they neared the head I could hold back no longer, the intensity was too much and I busted. Thick ropes of cum rained down upon them, each girl lapped up as much as they could. My release had started a game of hungry hungry cumsluts. I wasn't keeping score, but I'm pretty sure I won.

Recovery time, just a few minutes, was all I needed for round two. We all lay there, one girl under each of my arms. My hands playfully tugging at nipples until I was back at full power. I figured one good fuck and we should be done. That first load felt really draining and I could not guarantee a round three. Strategy was crucial to make both of them happy with what I had left. I donned a condom and positioned our guest to go down on Monica's pussy while I would fuck her doggy style. As she began to lap I could see in Monica's eyes she was enjoying the oral of the orient. Gently I pushed into my first Asian cunt.

It held me in a warm embrace as I pumped her. Deeper and deeper I ventured in exploring her cock cave as deep as I could. Her skin was so soft as I bounced off of her repeatedly. She was tight for sure, her pussy desperately begging to be fed. This seed was not for her though, the home for it was laying down being brought to orgasm by a smooth silky tongue. The sounds of her finishing was the cue for me to blow my load. I withdrew and slid off my condom, ready to fire away at a moments notice. I ordered a command, " now you ride her face." She slid up, making friends with Monica's mouth, leaving her mound fully exposed. As the moans started up top I went in down low.

Dear god Monica was hot and tight. So much foreplay had created a monster, a pussy I could not contain myself in. I could hardly move, every wiggle so pleasurable it brought me to the brink. I looked up when I heard a short scream and saw our guest was cumming. At last I yielded, plunging deep inside I unleashed and fully flooded her womb. I shook, I shivered, I collapsed. As I rolled off, I saw the massive creampie I had left slowly rolling out of her. Instinctively our guest slid down and gently scooped out every drop. She might not have been much to look at but, that single moment of unsolicited eroticism made it all worth it.

    She left that day very happy she had came over and wanted to return. Monica and I talked about it and decided we wanted to pursue other opportunities. The sex had not been bad, but it was not good enough for a second helping. For months she messaged me on and off, wanting to be a piece on the side. A tempting offer, but I needed to focus on my goal. A side piece would make me lazy, even complacent. She refused to cease so I had to block her. I truly wish her nothing but the best.

CHAPTER EIGHT

The tale of the soggy sneakers

Winter was upon us and everything was going smoother than it had been going for some time. I was working five part time jobs, the only work I could find, to save up and go to EMT school. My girlfriend Monica and I were doing great, better than great. Our sex life was amazing, we never had arguments, and the puppy love stage was in full swing.

We had a difficult time trying to understand how we, a pair of horny misfits, managed to be so happy when we had no examples of non-fictional functioning relationships growing up. Her parents were on a one-way trip to divorce while mine seemed determined to stick it out until either one or the other died.

My father was a decent dad but he really dropped the ball in the husband department. One day, after twenty years of marriage, my father drove my mother to the emergency room. She was having a heart attack. He dropped her off and drove the fuck home, leaving her alone until I managed to visit later that night after my shift. I was truly surprised he shed a tear when she passed away.

This brings us to December 21st, a day that will forever haunt me. I had called off work, too exhausted from working the aforementioned five jobs to make it in. They were upset, called the cops and claimed I was psycho. I was awoken from my slumber to, "Honey, some people are here to see you." I fumbled down the stairs to find several officers inside my living room. They ushered me outside to ask some questions. Ask they did- "Do you know so-and-so?" and "Why were you going to hurt people?". The "Put your hands behind your back" was not a question.
There was no evidence against me- no video, no texts, only testimony from a coworker. There was no proof that I hadn't done what she had accused me of, however, and when I was unable to prove my innocence they took me away in handcuffs.

I spent 23 hours in the emergency room waiting for a bed. They had not yet charged me with a crime, so they could only have me involuntarily committed to 'protect society'. I'd never harm a fly unless it asked me to. They threw me in with the others, the people who really needed help.
These people wanted to do evil things, hurt themselves, or heard voices. It wasn't the kind of company I wanted to be around.

Day two had me shitting bricks. The smallest event had triggered an episode with a large woman. She had to be at least three hundred pounds, maybe more. A glass of water was spilled. Some got on her and she went into a rage. She picked up the table, which had to be about six feet across, and tossed it to the other side of the main activity area. I ran to the corner and fucking cried. It took three men to drug her and take her down.

The hospital stripped me of my safety and freedom. The county prison took my dignity as well. Over my 72-hour stay they had determined that since I was not crazy, logically, that I must be a violent terrorist and that they should prosecute me. Just what I always wanted to do- spend Christmas eve getting finger printed and tossed into the mental health unit of the county prison. They took my clothes, my phone, and my pride and brought me to my new home- MHU cell 1031.

I wasn't allowed clothing. They were of the opinion that somehow I could kill myself with a pair of jeans. I was given a smock that was as thick as two oven mitts sewn together, a blanket that matched, and a pair of paper-thin loafers. Nothing was allowed in your cell, no tv, no paper, nothing but your own thoughts. There were no windows and the lights never went out- they had to see you were still alive on the security camera. There was only one clock at the end of the hall, barely visible through the slot in the door known as the 'winkey hole'. I didn't even get a bed, I got a plastic sled with a hard foam pad. One star, do not recommend.

There was a cellmate with me in there, but even after three days we had not exchanged names. This guy belonged there, he had headbutted a cop and threatened to kill his whole family. Although he was covered head to toe in prison tattoos, he was really a nice guy to me. He truly believed my innocence and that alone made my time much more tolerable.

My second night in I finally got a shower and, to be honest, it's the best thing Santa has ever given me. Washing off five days of dirt restored my soul. The holiday meal was not bad. When you're on the inside the only thing keeping track of your time is the next meal. On Christmas we each got a little piece of cake with sprinkles on it, the only festive sight to be seen. It was the best thing we had until Mr.Bignose came in.

It was around 9 p.m. when all the commotion started. A man was being dragged into our block throwing the biggest hissyfit he possibly could. "Fuck this", "fuck that", "fuck you", etcetera was all he could muster as they manhandled him into his cell.

A soft voice rang out,"Hey, I think I know you." This voice belonged to the transvestite that occupied my neighboring cell at the time. There were several minutes of back and forth before the fucking bomb dropped.

"Hey, did anyone see if that guy had a big nose?"

Several voices echoed back a confirmation.

"Oh shit! I knew I recognized that voice! You tried to get me to suck your dick downtown but I told you to fuck off you big-nosed ugly motherfucker!"

Everyone, including myself, laughed for several minutes, jeering on Mr.Bignose well into the night until I eventually fell into a deep slumber.

I awoke the next morning to a loud rapping at the door. I figured one of us was in trouble and hoped it wasn't me. See, when you're in the mental health unit you have immunity from regular punishment. You are not deemed mentally competent and anything you do, up to and including violence, cannot increase your sentence. When was I going to get another opportunity like that? In the twenty-four hours since learning about the immunity I had taken full childish advantage. Every time a guard was walking up the hallway I would walk to the door, open the flap, and yell, "Help! Help! My penis is too big to fit in this cell!". I would then proceed to stick my dick through the winkey hole and wave it at them, bringing me tears of joy in that trying time.

A deep voice barked, "Labour, your bail has been posted and you will be released this evening."

I wanted to thank him, but by the time my brain processed what he has said he was long gone.

Roughly an hour after my last meal in the clink, I was removed from my cell and brought to a large counter. All of my possessions were returned to me: my clothes, shoes, wallet, keys, and cell phone. They moved me to a holding cell with five other men who were also waiting to be released. Everyone was chomping at the bit for freedom, announcing their plans for the second they got outside. From a fresh pack of cigarettes to an ice cold beer, everyone had their desires all planned out.

A lone female prisoner was escorted down the hall right past us and put into an opposing cell. She was very attractive and the wolf whistles and cat calls roared from our cell. What ended the banter was one of the men, the smallest of our group, finally speaking out. "Can you calm it down, please? That's my wife."

What a moment ago had been jovial celebration from brothers in bondage was now awkward silence. Everyone stared at their feet, feeling bad for what they had unknowingly done.
"So, kid-" the married man decided to break the silence, "-what are you gonna do when you get out?"
I looked him dead in the eye when I said, "I'm gonna go out and get fucked."
I was loved by all but the man who asked. I was king. I had the biggest balls in that fucking cell and I made sure everyone knew it. Little did I know how right my statement truly was.

I was cast out in the darkness on a cold December night with nothing but my keys and a cell phone which was almost out of battery. The slightest drizzle fell as I walked down the release ramp back into society. The other men scattered in all directions, headed towards their goals. Where was my goal? I had no idea if my girlfriend would ever speak to me again after getting locked up. My balls were sore. I had been unable to find the private time I needed in either facility and so had not cum in 6 days. I opened up the online classifieds and began my search as I walked towards home. I knew full well I was going to cum that night, the only question now was who was gonna help me.

I found myself gazing at a picture of a beautiful

woman. We are talking a solid nine out of ten, well out of my league. There was also a man, quite handsome, that came along with her. The ad seemed too good to be true, they were local and hosting. They wanted a guy my age to come over and dick down the wife. Only catch was he was not to cum, the husband was to milk whoever came over. At the time I had no idea what that meant, nor did I care. I was willing to do that and more to cum that night. I responded, and within minutes I had the address. The drizzle turned to a steady downpour as I headed over.

A quick stop at a corner store gave me the protection I needed. A few minutes later and I was at their front door. I had always heard the phrase, "fuck like I just got out of jail," and was eager to experience it for myself. Days of sensual thoughts had built up a significant amount of pressure. If this woman was real and looked anything like the photo? Lord have mercy.

Welcoming me inside was the fine looking Spanish man from the ad. I was led to the couch where his lovely wife sat. The pictures had not done her justice, she was even more beautiful in person. She had a slender figure with plump perky breasts, shoulder-length curly hair, and amber eyes. The gameplan was set- I was to fuck her to my heart's content as long as I did not cum, once ready he would come in and milk me while I ate her out. Silly me still thought he knew what that meant, I was wrong. Some treasures come with a curse that you don't realize until it's in your hands.

The drizzle-turned-downpour had me soaked pretty much all over. The only dry remaining part of my entire body was the inside of my shoes and socks. As she disrobed and took her position on the couch I followed suit. I piled my clothes up right at the side of the couch and slid my shoes off right beside the pile. After a quick once over I mounted that piece of ass with passion. The deep lustful ache within me needed satisfied.

Every light kiss on the neck or pinch of the nipple made her hotter and wetter. She was so warm, her hole as inviting as any. My body was cold from the rain and her heat enveloped me. I could smell the faintest hint of her sex, an intoxicating aroma. I rolled the condom on as she fondled my very swollen balls. The penetration was slow and cautious. I was a man of my word and was determined not to cum until I was made to cum.

Over the next few minutes this went from making love to a hardcore fuck- tightly squeezing her throat as my pelvis slammed hers, slapping her tits, and flicking her clit. I flipped her around and put her on her knees. Doggy style was gonna make her cum, I just knew it. I went in hard and deep, with each penetration and withdrawal I felt her swell tighter and tighter until she tensed up. I felt the heat of her pussy juices gushing out as I popped out desperately trying not to join her. It was time, I needed milked, whatever that meant.

She called for him and laid on her back, her pussy spread wide and ready to make friends with my face. I stood at the end of the couch, clothes at my feet, bent at a ninety degree angle. I figured this was the best angle for him to tug me, I did not have to watch.

I felt him approach from behind but tried not to notice. I buried myself in my work, this swollen pussy was my focus tonight. I felt a gentle toss of my balls and a firm grip at the base of my shaft. I knew all I had to do was cum and I could go. The plan was to just keep doing what I'm doing, pretend he's not there, blow fast, and then bounce. Gently a finger ran up and down my shaft, I could feel the cool air flow around my pulsing manhood. Her heavy breathing kept me going. The reminder I was making someone happy, that I had value, even if it was only as a sextoy.

The gentle tickle of a slippery finger encircled my asshole. I was willing to submit to a finger in my ass if that's what this guy had in mind, anything to make me release this ungodly amount of pressure. It wasn't too bad, it kind of hurt but not enough to distract me from my task at hand. I felt it go deep inside me, my brain still not understanding what was going on. My only thought was, "Man, this guy has big fucking fingers!" That thought quickly vanished when I felt a hand on each side of my waist. That wasn't a finger.

The pressure inside me was intense, the orgasm was definitely building fast. He pumped in and out of me like I had done to his wife mere minutes ago. He was however, in much better shape then I and it felt like he was fucking me harder then I had fucked his wife. So dramatically that night had changed. I went from the guy with the biggest balls in the room, to getting fucked by the guy with even bigger balls. I had made it through prison without dropping the soap only to lose my ass cherry on the way home.

My tongue whipped like a whirlwind, throwing her into a quivering orgasm. Her thighs locked tight around my head. I could hold it no longer and began to violently ejaculate blindly. My knees gave out as six days worth of cum came rocketing out. It actually hurt a bit deep down inside as I emptied everything I had. The pressure relieved behind me as he slid out, leaving me kneeling in a pile of my own satisfaction. As I looked down I realized what I had done. My shoes, the only dry part of my attire, had managed to catch literally every drop that had come out. I was too sore and too tired to care. After composing myself I got dressed, thanked them for a lovely evening , and made for the door.

I walked a mile home, cowboy style in the rain. My battery, left with only two percent left, had just enough juice to look up what milking was. From the description I found it is typically done with a finger. A man has a finger stuck up his ass and someone massages the prostate. This is like squirting, but for men. That son of a bitch played me like a fiddle. He took what he wanted, but in all fairness I would have done it again to get another crack at that wife of his. My phone went dark, I looked up to see my house off in the distance. I went straight up to my room and immediately passed out; no shower, no washcloth, still wearing my soggy sneakers.

CHAPTER NINE
A hole is a hole

Six months had passed since I was released and overall things were going pretty good. Monica had stayed by my side through the whole ordeal. She had even accepted my proposal for marriage. Without her unending love I would not have had the heart to carry on. Strings of temporary jobs payed the bills but money was always tight. The trial and bail had taken every cent I had saved up to go to EMT school. The charges against me barred me from that profession for life.

Monica and I had a relationship that became the envy of all our friends. Two horny young adults highly skilled in the art of glandular combat made for some very happy times indeed. To add to this, on my days off I was able to browse the online classified adding notch after notch with what little fluids I had left in me. My body was deeply into "repopulate the world," mode. I was unable to contain certain biological processes for more then forty eight hours without extreme discomfort. This was not an issue, until

Monica told me of an upcoming trip she was taking that would have her away from me for three whole days.

I tried, I honestly did. Originally I had wanted to save myself for her. She would have gotten quite the bath with three days rushing out all at once. Day one was fine, I went about it as usual. Day two, on the other hand, was a dark day. My libido was on a hair trigger and even the slightest stimuli was gonna set me off.

As I parked my car after a long day at work, a woman pushing a stroller walked by me. She had a ridiculously fat ass that her yoga pants clung to for dear life. One of her kids threw something on the ground. The loving mother bent down to retrieve it, unknowingly giving me a wonderful view of not only her ass, but her clearly visible camel toe. I was hypnotized by it, just a hair too much to get out of my mind. I felt the ache within me. The fuse had been thoroughly lit.

Hunting for hours and coming up empty handed is depressing. Your catch could be just out of sight, waiting to be taken home. Every email I sent was left unreplied to. Every dating site had no one online. I seemed to be the only one in town looking to have fun that night. There was, however, one email that reached by inbox. It was a 'you scratch my back, I'll scratch yours' proposal. A genuine offer to receive oral sex, the caveat being I also had to return the favor. I tried for another hour before I caved in and wrote back. I was far too sore to continue the search with my balls ready to burst. Humbly, but with much hesitation, I accepted his offer.

    For me, sex is a physical act not necessarily linked to attraction. Many people I have fucked had not gotten me all hot and bothered. Heterosexuality was definitely my preference, with the concept of bisexuality being more of a curiosity. I could not say for sure whether I could do it, for I had never done it. This was the first time I willingly walked into a situation knowing I would solely be with a man. Fear filled my heart, I have no idea why. Perhaps it was because I was going to be an actual participant this time and not just bent over a couch and raw dogged.

    The meeting spot was a dark back porch with a shadowed figure upon it. If I had ever been to a shady meet up, this was the one. A cloud of smoke masked him even further. I kept my distance until I got my bearings, cautious as I approached. He opened the screen door and walked inside, telling me to follow him. This, for me, was just so difficult to do. I felt like I was throwing in the towel, like I had settled. Once I walked in, there was no going back. My mind was telling me no.
    My legs didn't listen.

    His home was lavishly furnished with all kinds of trinkets. The treasure trove of things he collected in his travels really brought the room together. The room was dominated by a large tropical aquarium swimming with life. Their vibrant colors really drew the eye. At least I can look back and say this went down in a classy place, not in the likes of a bus station bathroom or a viewing booth at an adult video store. Not enough to hold my head up high, mind you, but high enough I'd be able to tell what shirt you have on.

My heartbeat thundered in my ears as I prepared to do what was agreed. Phil, the man who had humbly let me into his home, and was willing to let me in his mouth as well, stood by a plush recliner. His calmness bothered me, my adrenaline telling me fight or flight, neither a logical option. The only thing I had to fear was fear itself. That, and of course finding out I really liked it and discovering that I was, in fact, gay. Highly unlikely, but who could say at that point. All I knew was that I had not despised being fucked in the ass. Maybe I'd like this too.

He gave me the choice, I could give first or I could receive first. That question was one I had to think about. Both had their benefits, but one sounded more my style. If I gave first, I could then receive and retreat. Going first had the prospect of a smooth dash to the finish line. I told him my choice, his sweatpants hit the floor and he took his position. He was still so calm. I think he may have been amused by my nervousness. I fell to my knees and accepted my fate.

Phil was well-on in years, maybe mid fifties to early sixties. His flesh was wrinkled, his spirit willing, but his body too feeble to act. I gave it my all, tugging and sucking at his phalic relic between his thighs. Trying my best to appease my host. His balls were saggy, just as you would expect them to be. I was on my knees, fully submitting to him and attempting to suck a golf ball through a garden hose. He let me go on for about five minutes before it was made clear that his Viagra had not worked that night. I offered to leave, unsatisfied. He refused and told me to sit down on the chair.

That old man gave it his all, but his experience seemed to rival mine for all the skill level displayed. I was as eager to cum as I could be, my balls were swollen to the breaking point and all he had to do was give some meaningful stimulation and I would have erupted. I knew he wanted me to blast my soul down his awaiting throat. I was not going to leave here without emptying my swollen balls. I decided, right then and there, that men would count too. Regardless of what was between his legs, he still deemed me fuckable. Thats all I ever wanted to prove. All that needed to happen was one of us was going to have to finish. With his penis out of commission, that left only me.

I got his attention and had him back up. Standing there my hand took over, a grand improvement over the stimulation from seconds ago. The pressure rose as I could feel myself getting close to the edge. Poor Phil deserved to be whitewashed for his valiant efforts. His face awaited my load, a smile stretched from ear to ear. I told him to squeeze my balls. I wanted him to be a part of the grand finale.

As he squeezed I thought of Monica that night at the park. That first look deep into her eyes. It was the most arousing memory I had. That instant all of that pent up testosterone came flooding out. My hips bucked and my cock pulsed uncontrollably as I doused this man from forehead to beard. My pulsing rod tried its best to aim but with that amount of pressure it was more of a skeetshoot.

When the streams finally stopped he unleashed my balls and slid his hand firmly up my hyper sensitive shaft, eager to get that last drop out before I departed. As he licked my baby batter off his hand I carefully put my throbbing member back in my pants and said farewell. I took one last look back as I opened the screen door. He had turned on the TV and sat down in his chair. When I left him he was still wearing a face mask of my seed, gently lapping the cum in his beard.

As I drove home, I tried to think over what I had just done in my mind. I had released, but I did not get the same joy as if my target had been female. I could now say, without a shadow of a doubt that I was not gay. Throughout my life I had always had my preconceived notions about those who chose to have relations with their own gender. I had assumed they were failures, that they had given up or just were not worthy of the other gender. Phil honestly broke all of those stereotypes for me. From the lavishness of his home I could tell he was no failure. The confidence he displayed well overshadowed my own. He simply wanted a man instead of a woman.

Two days later Monica returned. They decided to stay an extra day which allowed me to swell to capacity once more. Although Monica and I were open I was still nervous about telling her about my encounter. It took me three days to work up the courage. I hadn't needed to worry, she was understanding and kind. For once, someone understood me for what I was. This was something I personally needed to learn to do. What once was a negative opinion of homosexuals became neutral and over time became positive. The group which I once ridiculed I now respected. For me, having sex with a man was a choice, an option. For them it was the only option. I was never successfully with a single male after that. I was with couples, but never went all the way with just a man again.

CHAPTER TEN
Sleazyanna

    Infidelity has broken up its fair share of relationships. Just the suspicion of the act is often enough to pull previously close couples apart. A great benefit of an open relationship is that this risk is pretty much nullified. We still have basic rules that, if broken, will raise an argument. Over the years we have had very few misunderstandings, most of which did not even pertain to sex. Jealousy is a tricky mistress and can strike at any moment. The definition of cheating is different from person to person. What if your husband kissed another woman? Your wife was holding hands with another man? Your girlfriend spends the night at a guy's house? Your fiancee buys another woman a sex toy? All of these things and many more can drive a massive wedge in the trust of any relationship. If you are strong, and you both truly love one another, you will pull through. So far Monica and I have had zero serious disputes and I could not be happier.

    I was really killing it with the online classifieds.

You know you've truly made it when you get hate mail on the daily and everyone tries to pull your ads down as soon as they are live. A group of guys kept targeting me, deleting my ads as fast as they could. Try as they might, though, responses kept getting through. I had my target audience and I was relentless in letting them know I was the one to choose. My confidence won them over. My post not made up stories or empty promises, but honesty on what I had done, what I can do today, and what I will do in the future.

    I offered several 'services'. Some ads were in search of single mothers for the sheer fact that life kind of sucked for them . Being a single mom has to be a struggle for most, I looked to alleviate the stress and bring forth the joy. Other ads looked for virgins only. A very small margin of those online were in fact virgins with no other alternative. My charm and compassionate description lured a good number of them in. My main fetish, my real bread and butter, was teaching women to squirt. I didn't know if I was the world's best, but I was definitely a contender for the belt. The results spoke for themselves, if you could do it - I would make it happen.

    Not long after I had posted an ad, one of several I posted that Wednesday morning, lightning struck. A woman wrote me, responding to my ad regarding female ejaculation. Her story got me all hot and bothered. She claimed to have squirted only once before. A carnival had come to town and she had hooked up with a carnie inside one of the rides while it was down for maintenance. She was a cute-sounding southern Jezebel with a baby on board. Her pregnancy, seven months along, was making her extremely horny. Her boyfriend was unwilling or unable to satisfy her. She was a damsel in distress. I had to come to her aid.

Discretion was a must, her neighbors could not find out about her escapade or they would rat her out. I met her at a nearby bank. Her looks matched the brief description she had sent. She was only four foot nine, a tiny thing compared to me. Her long blonde hair was cute, a pink highlight ran down one side of it. Her breasts were swollen from the pregnancy, she did not know her current size but the last bra that fit her was a 36 C. Rolling up I noticed her warm motherly glow and that baby belly. Something about pregnant women has always done something for me and I was excited to finally have my first. Not long into the car ride home I began to feel her up, her body fully submitting to my will. Her swollen breasts were hyper sensitive, so much so that every bounce from a pothole got her more and more aroused. Her face was fully flushed by the time we got back to my place.

At this point I owned my own home. Monica was at work so my guest and I had the home to ourselves. I had a special room at the top of the stairs for just this occasion. A loveseat was inside. Now, the loveseat is the perfect sexual furniture in my honest opinion. The loveseat is wide enough to spread out and eat pussy or receive head, but small enough to control the entire area. The sides are at waist height, perfect to bend someone over.

A towel was laid down and we went over the gameplan. She stripped, finally revealing her most sensitive areas. Her swollen breasts drew your eyes up but her cunt drew your eyes down. A cute little landing strip was all that remained of the hair on her sex, her bubbly clit and the thin lips of her pussy were the plane coming in for a landing. It was truly a sight to behold. I got on my knees and leaned in to get my first taste. It was like opening up a dishwasher, the steamy heat coming off would have fogged up a pair of glasses. I swirled my tongue in every direction, making a true meal of her cunt. It was lunchtime and this snack would have to suffice.

Her previous squirt from the description was small and weak, what I planned to deliver was the polar opposite. I took my time, drew her closer and closer to orgasm. Her fingers dug deep into the couch as her panting and moans intensified, the occasional profanity crossing her lips. My fingers, chomping at the bit to begin their handy work started sliding up and down her thighs. Just then the phone rang, it was her boyfriend.

The sex had an intermission. Two minutes of her talking to her man, giving some fake story about her whereabouts. From the side of the conversation that I was able to hear he was a good guy. I tried to press those thoughts out of my mind. As she hung up I immediately resumed my task. My left hand had found her tight tunnel, my right had found her breast. Casually I felt her up, playing with her nipple as I got her ready to finish. I felt a warm wet sensation up at my hand but could not see what was going on past her baby belly. I pulled my hand down to investigate, she had begun to lactate.

Unsure of what to do I swapped hands, deciding her other breast needed an equal amount of attention. I began to rake her from within. Her g-spot swollen and rough. Every drag bringing her closer and closer to the edge. My method was systematic with the intention to make the receiver feel orgasmic. I felt the first convulsion of her baby tunnel. As she started locking down on my hand I sucked hard on her clit and squeezed firmly on her breast. My face was getting water boarded by this slutty fire hydrant. Every time she unlocked I began raking again. Her legs swung around and locked around my head. She pulled my hair and shook as her orgasm overwhelmed her.

The towel was definitely in need of a good wash. The fabric slightly moist beneath it. I let her rest a minute while I readied myself and tried to work through how we were going to do this. Usually I would bend them over the couch and fuck them until they were raw. I did not want to harm the baby so as I slid on a condom I had her lay on the floor. It was the only position I could think of that offered me a great view of her. Even after she dried off she was still so wet I easily slipped in. Her cock cave was swollen and tight, though, with just enough pussy fat to give you a hug as you bottomed out.

I was cautious and careful for I had never done this before with a pregnant girl. I did not want to hurt her or the baby. It felt nice plunging deep in and back out. I got into a rhythm that made her cum. Every few minutes she would finish and while she finished I would recover. I was running out of stamina when once again, the phone rang.

It was her man, again, once more cock bocking me via cell phone. This time, however, the conversation got a lot more intimate. I was still inside her, dumbfounded that she had picked up a second time. Phrases came out that had not come out before, that revealed that she was lying about her situation. I wasn't just fucking some guys girlfriend, it was his fiancee. Who the fuck would be so sick as to lead someone on like that? Saying," of course I want to marry you why would you say something like that?" while having another man's penis inside of you.

As she neared the end of the call I began to slowly start again, her man on the other end unaware of the deeds. The only giveaway was a slight hesitation in her responses. When the call finally ended she was relieved to let loose her moans and whimpers once more. I wanted this to end, it just didn't feel right anymore. Now that I knew what I was doing things were different.

An engagement is not something I take lightly, it is a true commitment to another person. One that should not be violated. He deserved to know the truth, but how could he? I figured if he called again I would say something loudly while she was on the line. It was the least I could do for the poor guy.

Pressure was building, although there was no longer an emotional connection I was still inside a hot pulsing cunt begging for seed. We had not discussed the exit strategy prior to starting and my mind was full of ideas. Would it be best to splatter her leaking tits and make a cum-based cocktail? Maybe I should fill her lying mouth. Ever the gentleman, I was kind enough to ask. Her response was not specific enough to make a determination on what was okay and what wasn't. I interpreted it the best I could. Her answer of "doesn't matter" did not specifically rule out cumming inside.

Quickly I pulled out, ripped off the condom and without wasting a second plunged back in. This load had to be special, it had a purpose. The plan was to now flood her with every drop of seed I could. If I was lucky, hopefully her man would smell it and save himself.

I began to go deep, deepest I had been. Her legs on my shoulders as I bashed against her cervix. Her face scrunched every time and then went back to expressions of delight. I felt her pussy lock up on me, trying to squirt but she had nothing left in the tank. As I came it contracted pulling out every little sperm it could. A shiver ran down my spine as I held her close. She was looking at me, confused.
"Did you just cum inside of me?" She asked.
"You said anywhere?" I replied.
She was not a happy camper.

She quickly got up and was headed for the bathroom when the phone rang. Surprise, surprise- it was her man, again. This call was short, apparently he was on his way home and she lied saying she was already home. We had to hurry. She wiped what she could off with the towel and threw her clothes back on.

"If we hurry we can get me back before he gets home. I can get a shower and start some laundry and he will be none the wiser."

"Sounds like a plan," I replied, and with that I ran downstairs to grab my keys. Time was of the essence. As I reached for the door I heard the lock. Monica was home early.

Quickly I filled her in as my newly-filled house guest came down the stairs. She walked past us both with a smile and headed through the door on her way to the car. "Did you cum on her?" Monica asked.

"No, why?" I replied.

"You can really smell it on her breath, then." She said with a slight giggle as she sat down and turned on the TV. I did not lie, really. She asked if I came on her. I did not cum on her, I came *in* her.

We drove with a strong sense of urgency and were a few minutes ahead of schedule. We talked as we drove and more and more I leaned towards the side of her man. I was not about to flat out tell her this, seeing as how she had been kind enough to come over that day. We were roughly half way back when she realized she had forgotten her key at my house. Fuck.

We pulled a one-eighty but there was no way she was going to make it home in time now. I dropped her off at the same spot I had picked her up at. She left without a word. She remembered her key this time, the only thing left behind was a wet spot on the seat. As she walked away you could clearly see the outline of her leaking gash through the sweatpants- the mixture of our fluids draining as she walked.

She messaged me later saying she had been found out. He was waiting for her when she got home and was not happy. He ended up kicking her out and she had to fly back down south to live with her family. Her final message, "you were worth it," hit home. Someone out there saw value in me, more than I could see in myself. None of the rules I started out with seemed to matter to me anymore. The condom came off, my lustful urge to defile her overruled my logical reasoning. I had caused harm but in the name of good. My valor had transformed me to a vigilante of vaginal based justice. Deep down I knew what I had done was right.

CHAPTER ELEVEN
Inside the furnace

Sex can be a beautiful union or downright disgusting. Both men and women can be pigs behind closed doors. Over the years I have heard many phrases that I did not approve of. This *is* the world of casual sex mind you, but it does not have to be so vulgar. Countless men have said, "I would eat the corn from her shit." Some went as far as to say they would "lick her shitter like an apple fritter." I am far from done with this way of life so the list continues to grow. Just the other day a man gave me a pick up line I will never forget. "I want to suck a fart out of your ass like a bong rip." He really thought that one would win me over. For fuck's sake people show some class- you're better then that, I hope.

Autumn was once again in full swing. The leaves were turning their vibrant shades of red, orange and yellow. The nights had just started to cool again, with temperatures in the high fifties to low sixties and a gentle breeze. School was back in session which meant opportunities abounded.

Every so often I saw college girls on the sites I frequented. They typically were looking for things greater then I. Things I just could not offer. Some wanted a big black cock, others wanted money for school or even a place to stay. They popped up after a month or so, ever so sporadic like bolts of lightning. You just had to be in the right place when it struck.

I ended up finding her on a dating site where she had put "up for anything," as one of her preferences. I earnestly contacted her with full honesty and decency. I complimented her looks, making sure she knew just how amazing her ass truly was. Slowly I began to convey my goal was to teach her to squirt. Through a conversation encompassing close to a hundred messages- I convinced her that not only was I the one she should choose, but also, she needed this to happen *tonight* at her place. Her pictures made her look rather attractive. A chubby brunette with a decent sized bust. Truly her greatest feature was behind her, a real pawg if I ever saw one. Better than I expected with how willing she was to be with me. I did not want to keep her waiting so I hurriedly got dressed and made my way downstairs. I grabbed my sex bag, kissed my now-fiancee Monica goodbye, and was off.

This is the first encounter in the book where I have used the phrase "sex bag" and I am guessing you may be confused. Over my career the tastes of my clientele as well as myself have evolved. I grew tired of being ill prepared for certain situations. Inside this bag I had pretty much everything I needed to satisfy the desires of whomever happened to respond to one of my ads: condoms, both latex and lambskin for those with allergies in hearty supply, towelettes, lube, a remote-controlled egg with batteries, and even a couple butt plugs made the cut. Several pairs of rubber gloves were inside to shield sensitive love tunnels from my rough callused hands. A flogger for the naughty ones. Sex toy cleaner and last, but surely not least, was Ole Reliable.

Ole Reliable was the bargain of the century. Originally purchased for the low cost of only $7.99, it proved to be the most lethal tool in my arsenal. Made of firm rubber, it was over seven inches long and had the girth of a soda can. This thing kicked ass and took names. With my arm at the helm, this massive man meat made every pussy fall to ruin in its wake. If I couldn't wear you out, he took over. Ever willing to completely demolish anything in its path.

I parked a block away, striding up proudly to claim my prize. It was not often I got invited to their place, more often I picked them up and brought them to mine. A person is always more relaxed in their own home, more able to release and truly appreciate what I bring to the table. The walk did me good, it got my heart pumping. I had ridden my motorcycle over and my fingers were nearly numb from the ride. The rest of me was pretty cold too but that short walk seemed to warm me up well enough. As I reached the destination I saw the door creak open and she welcomed me in.

"We need to be quiet, my roommates are asleep,"

she whispered as she shut the door.

"Lead the way." I replied as I gave her a once over- paying special attention to her incredibly fat ass.

A quick slap on that badonkadonk was all I could get in before she headed up the stairs. Her ass a bouncing target for me to chase. We climbed not one, not two, not even three, but *four* full flights of stairs. The view was definite motivation to pursue her. I became all hot and bothered, but it was not just me getting hotter. Each step felt a little warmer then the last. This femme fatale was leading me up the steps of hell.

As we reached our summit I was out of breath. The stairs apparently did not phase her at all. Perhaps conditioned by their frequent use or maybe she was so excited to have me over that she had extra energy. The siren lured me to her bedside as her clothes hit the floor. Each article she slid off showed more of her tender flesh beneath. I followed her lead, not wanting to disappoint my host. Her stripping was to arouse and entice me. Mine was for sheer survival- the window was shut, there was no fan, and her comforter was thick and warm. No relief from the heat in sight.

Seductive eyes and a cute grin drew me in. She leaned forward and popped me into her mouth, the vacuum she made was more then enough pressure to get me rock hard . I wanted to hold off, not be a two-pump Charley like the rest of the men she had recently been with. She bobbed up and down, I became well acquainted with the back of her throat. Her skills were above average, good enough to make most men bust uncontrollably. Her mouth, although warm, actually felt cooler then the room we were in. I could feel sweat starting to run down my back as she popped off my now rigid fuck stick.

   Not one to receive and not return I buried my face between her thighs. She was a bigger girl, her pussy well fed. I was being smothered as I dove in attacking her clit like a punching bag. My tongue willing to go ten rounds until she couldn't take it anymore. Her moans grew louder as she ran her fingers through my hair. A few small circles was all she needed to climax. Suddenly she pulled me forward, smashing my nose into her without warning.
   "FFUUUCCCCKKKKK!" She roared as she let go of me.

   Happy my nose was not broken I continued the charge, grabbing the gloves and lube from my bag. My hands made their way in without resistance. Her cunt coaxed me in, wanting everything I had to offer. I could feel her gspot swelling as I raked over it. Faster and faster I
   dragged against just the right spot, keeping her wanting as I balanced her on the edge of orgasm. She began to empty the tank, her face in shock as my fingers did their magic. Panting as over and over again her pussy convulsed and forced whatever liquid it could out. Her body shook hard as she went from stream, to splash, all the way down to barely noticeable. She lay back, shaking, conquered by my hands.

The only thing wetter then her was me. The temperature continued to rise to dangerous levels. The only reprieve from the heat was the glorious puddle she had made pooling around my knees. I noticed she had begun to sweat as well, a true sign that things were *indeed* getting hotter. I needed to nut and get out fast before I was boiled alive.

I retreated to my bag and slid on a condom ready to charge into battle. Impressed that somehow it had not melted in this god forsaken inferno. I was now ribbed for her pleasure and going in. I ordered her onto her stomach which was, for me, a no-brainer. She would not see me sweating so badly, her amazing ass would be front and center view, and (most importantly) she would be breathing in the opposite direction. Her breath did not smell but it was still hot and I had to take what opportunities I could. I approached her voluptuous ass, clearly her best feature, and got ready to mount. Her cunt was *ablaze*. Her pussy radiated heat, even wrapped around me like an anaconda trying to squeeze the life out of me. At least with a cunt like this I would be done fast.

First insertion I plunged as deep as I could, feeling every inch of what this cock cave had to offer. Slowly, I began to rock in and out establishing my rhythm. The pressure on my shaft was intense and my balls ever-sogently swung and slapped her meaty thighs with every thrust. Her legs were pressed firmly together and the sight of me bouncing off her ass was heaven.

Sadly, the room still felt like hell.

I started to cramp. Sweat was pouring off of me, some falling on her back as our bodies slammed together. I began to feel dizzy, my stomach uneasy. I picked up the pace, determined to finish no matter the cost. Loud claps echoed around the room as her ass splashed off me over and over again. I was no longer sure if I was leaving there with another notch or leaving in an ambulance. She was getting sore. Her moans had begun to turn into whimpers. I needed to finish fast for both our sakes.

She was soaked, no longer able to bear the heat either. This was no longer a booty call, this had transformed into a hate fuck. I spun her around, laying her on her back and putting those legs over my shoulders. This view of her mound aroused me- her clit a cute little jelly bean down below. I leaned forward and grabbed her throat, locking on without missing a beat in my ballad of vaginal destruction. Her eyes met mine, she was nervous but definitely excited by it. I could feel her pussy convulsing hard around me, unable to cum anymore. It was finally my turn.

I looked her dead in the eyes, my hand still holding firmly on her throat.

"I am about to cum. You are going to swallow every drop. Understood?" I barked at her.

I began to thrust harder, she winced in pain.

"UNDERSTOOD???" I was no longer asking. She nodded what little she could and with that, I released her from my grasp.

I quickly withdrew and she fell to her knees, ready to accept her fate. I barely had time to get the condom off before I erupted. Her soft lips wrapped around me as the pulsing commenced, my balls determined to empty themselves. Ten seconds later it was finally over. She stayed locked on until she was sure I was done. When she finally popped off she stuck out her tongue with pride to show she did good. She did do good, I didn't want good, I wanted perfection. A lone drop had spilled and landed on her chest. As I pointed it out a look of fear overtook her. Quickly she tried to lick it up but it was too late.

"Get on the bed," I ordered.

She cautiously got back on the bed. She was on all fours in full submission. Her ass waved nervously in the air as she buried her face in the pillow. I could hardly see through my sweat as I walked to my bag to grab what I needed: some lube, the flogger, and Ole Reliable.

I took a few good cracks at her with the flogger. Each time she flinched and each time I cracked it a little harder. She was already getting sore but I wanted to
leave her unable to continue. Carefully I brushed ole reliable from head to shaft with lube. Even though her pussy was still nice and wet, ole reliable would find a dry spot if there was one. I gave her one command as what little fluid was left in my body dripped from my forehead onto the floor.

"The safeword is pineapple," and with that I began to work Ole Reliable inside her, stretching her to her limits.

Deep breaths escaped her as I pushed her cunt to capacity. Any larger and I would not have been able to get it in at all. As I sped up her moans turned into yelps; the toy reaching the deepest parts of her pussy with every plunge. She was cumming so hard she could not take it anymore.

The toy ripped out of my hands as a deafening "PINEAPPLE", filled the room.

Shocked, I sat down beside her. Her cunt was fully locked around the toy as she held her position. I looked at her, she was tapped out, her mascara was running down her face.

I leaned in and whispered, "I thought you said we had to be quiet." A few seconds later, a loud thud filled the room as she released the toy. Finally I could head out.

I could barely pull my shirt on I was so wet. My pants felt like a true burden to get past my kneecaps. Dizzy and cramping but not defeated I packed my bag and headed for the stairs. My legs, more jelly than bone, could barely support me. She was unable to do the stairs in her condition and told me to show myself out. I happily obliged, I knew I had pushed her to her limits. I only stopped once during my descent. I was at the top of the stairs where the thermostat caught my eye. Ninety four fucking degrees. I fumbled down the stairs and out the front door. The cool air was like a tidal wave washing over me. I was like a new man, dehydrated of course, but new nonetheless.

After walking a block to my motorcycle I hopped

on with a sense of accomplishment and pride. I rode to the nearest gas station recalling all the messages we had sent back and forth. That was what she wanted, and I was lucky enough to be the one to deliver. I ended up chugging two sports drinks at the pump before riding

    home. This was not my easiest notch and very easily could have gone south. Had I passed out who knows where I would be right now. Would I have continued down this path or given up right then and there?

    The quest was half over, she was notch twenty five.

CHAPTER TWELVE
The Mermaid

Each person has their own set of both limits and expectations behind closed doors. Some fancy nothing more then a cuddle while others need to be whipped raw to get the same pleasure. Although I myself have been judged for my preferences under the covers I have never, nor will I ever judge someone for what gets them off. Over the years there have been many things I have found to enjoy by being open minded. Don't knock it till you try it guys, there are things in this world you should experience and you only find them through exploration. Judge not others for their fetishes, different strokes for different folks.

Being a manwhore is kind of like being a fisherman. Everyday you head out with your net and cast it over the side. You plop your line in the water and hope something takes a nibble. With a nibble you can sink the hook and reel it in if you've got the hutzpah. Some days you will have a bountiful harvest and others your net shall be bare. Deep down your really looking to hook something special. One day you pull up your net, not believing what is right infront of you. It flails and gets away, swimming back into the deep. No one believes you, but you know what you saw. You know what you had, and you know it got away. Even though no one believes you - you tell that tale until you die.

Her name was Ericka. Her neon green hair reminded me of seaweed and she always wore a pearl necklace just a shade too big for her. Fresh out of high school and headed down a dark path is where I found her. I saw her post an ad, looking for someone to show her anything and everything behind closed doors. Whether it was my cool calm demeanor or my concern for her welfare that made her choose me I will never know. This girl was a rebel, just looking for someone to give a shit about her for once.

Her punk rock attire, piercings, tattoos, and most of all that green hair - all screamed for attention. As I got to know I learned of her rocky past. She was in and out of foster care most of her life, never receiving a sense of belonging to any particular family. Never staying more then a year and really building a bond. She felt like she was all alone. I tried to comfort her, show her I could be a friend as well as a mentor. She humbly accepted my offer.

The majority of my notches were from one time hookups but on occasion the involvement continued past the first meeting. I was never really looking for an ongoing thing, but when someone was willing to learn I was willing to teach. Ericka did not want to be used.

She wanted an ongoing education in the art of fornication. Someone to guide her along the vanilla and not so vanilla ways of the bedroom. I taught her everything I knew over the next several weeks.

Our first meeting was pretty vanilla. Her attractive young figure was treated like a delicacy. She was not a virgin, but everything other then missionary was new to her. She wanted a taste of the dark side, I obliged. That day her ass was spanked till it turned bright red. A fantasy she always had became fulfilled when she had me grab her by the ears and fuck her throat like a rag doll. Her throat was hot and yearning for my seed. I finished hard, everything shot down her throat. As she pulls me from her mouth she looks up, still holding my throbbing cock in her hand. Sliding slowly up and down, milking the last few drops from me and lapping them up with her tongue.
" Did I do good?" she asked.
" You were perfect," I replied. She wore a grin till I dropped her off that day.

Our second meeting was much more intense. What was once a slap tuned into the crack of a belt. She wanted abused, tormented even . Much darker then I had ever gone before, even with Monica. The fucking got brutal. When her cunt could take no more I turned to her ass. She had always wanted it up the ass but wanted someone who knew what they were doing to be her first. Her ass cherry is one I will never forget.

She was thin, but also on the taller side. Close to five eleven if I had to wager. When I bent her over the

loveseat I had to rock on the balls of my foot to get the right angle. Even with enough lube her ass was locked up tight. I made my way inside, as gentle as I could. I began to fuck her ass ever so slowly. A soft voice escaped her, a message I needed to hear.
" Fuck me harder daddy!"

I picked up the pace, her tight little asshole clutching me tightly. I knew I was getting close to cumming, I could feel the pressure building deep within me. I reached for the belt, the same one that had left the welts now appearing on her ass. I made a leash and made her wear it. It was tight, but she could still breathe. Faster and faster my hips rocked, I could hold no longer. I pulled firmly on the leash and as she coughed it forced everything out of me and into her. As I finished I let go of the belt and ran all my nails down the center of her back. She grunted as she felt me pop out of her.

She was mine in every sense of the word. She wore my marks with pride and carried my seed within her. Following my orders were her one and only priority. Before she got up I got on top of her. Dominating her small frame and whispered ever so gently in her ear as I ran my finger up her ass crack.
"You lose one drop before you leave and I *will* whip you raw." Before heading to the car I checked, she was still dry. Good girl indeed.

As the mentor in that relationship everything fell on me. Whether this was a success or a failure was constantly on my shoulders. If I went too far, or even worse, not far enough, she may not want to see me again. If someone is uncomfortable you need to notice before they say something and try to remedy the situation as soon as possible. Never should someone suffer either physically or emotionally unless that is the sole directive of the play in question. I took the role very seriously, knowing one fuck up from me and this could all be over.

Our third meeting pushed both our comfort levels to their limits. We were going to play out in public with all the world to see. I had given Ericka specific instructions to wear some yoga pants. She had followed orders and wore a skin tight light gray pair. As we drove to our destination, a department store near the edge of town, I turned to my bag and withdrew the remote controlled egg and its remote. A quick test for function was done before I had her put the egg up inside her.

Ericka was a squirter, not much of one but she definitely did. Our plan was simple enough that it should have went off without a hitch. We were to walk around with me at the controls. If she felt like she was about to cum, she would squeeze my hand firmly and I would know to turn it off. That signal would draw no attention and no one would be the wiser. We agreed that as she and I walked to the car after leaving the store that I would crank it to max and she would cum all over herself. All while walking across the parking lot away from the general public. Kinky plan right?

We casually perused the aisles with no intention to

buy. When no one was around I would ramp up and ramp back down. Ericka was nervous but trusting. She knew I would never do anything to hurt her. As soon as someone was within earshot or within sight I backed it down. She was getting really aroused, her nipples clearly visible behind her tank top. Her flesh was blushed as we made our way to the register. We stopped and grabbed some sodas before getting in line. We held hands as I fiddled with the controls, bringing her to the edge of orgasm and then back down. Every time she squeezed I clicked it back off, waiting a minute then ramping back up.

Her sweaty hand held mine as she showed me her smile. The fact she was getting off in front of these people was really doing it for her. We were next two spaces back in line and I left it run on low. You couldn't hear it, but the egg was definitely going. We became next in line, I increased it to medium. Her breaths became slow and deep as she tried to contain herself. She had not squeezed , were we now at the register. I clicked it to high and as soon as I did you could hear it. That little motor screaming like a cell phone going off. She squeezed my hand tightly so I clicked the power button. Nothing happened.

I'm trying to keep my composure with the cashier and I am hitting the power off button over and over all the while Ericka is looking at me panicked. It won't shut off for some reason.
" Hey Ericka I think thats an important call you ought to go answer that," I say and with that she power walks towards the restroom in the front of the

store.

I finish my transaction and head over, upset at what had happened. I removed the remote from my pocket and found out the batteries had died. The little light at the top no longer illuminated when you pressed a key. This was all my fault, my cheap ass had used the batteries that came with it. What had I done?

Several minutes later Ericka came out with tears in her eyes. The hoodie she had on over her tank top now wrapped around her waist to shield her shame. The gray yoga pants had clearly captured the waterfall that had sprung from her fuck-hole. I was wrong, she really could squirt.

As much as I tried to explain that this was an accident I knew she did not believe me. I showed her the remote with the dead batteries but it was no use, the trust was thoroughly gone. I drove straight to her place to drop her off. She had not said a word the whole ride over. As she walked towards her door I cried out, " I truly am sorry, will I ever see you again?" Her response was a middle finger over her shoulder as she kept walking to the porch. She threw open the door and slammed it behind her, my mermaid had gotten away.

CHAPTER THIRTEEN
Not all about you

Sex, just like love, is a give and take relationship. Most often it is not a tit-for-tat kind of thing, but it is balanced enough to keep the peace. This is not to say you cannot be submissive or dominant, quite the contrary. A Sub derives pleasure from pleasing just as a Dom receives pleasure from either giving or denying satisfaction. The overall goal of my encounters was to deliver pleasure so grand they felt obligated to return the favor. In ninety percent of cases they did just that, happily so. But in that last ten percent we had people who wanted to receive but were not willing to reciprocate. Pillow princesses is their name and having all the fun is their game. The requirements to be one were relatively low, you had to have vagina, love being played with, and be extremely attractive. This girl had two of the three.

I had stumbled across her very early in the morning one day. She seemed lonely on her profile and a few messages got her just as interested in me as I was in her. A bigger girl but not excessively so. Close to five foot five with some decent tits. She was Latina and had the famous bubble butt. Her hair went just low enough to hide her knockers. She was cute, but was someone who would definitely be in my league if I was single.

She was nervous but willing to give me a shot. After finding a very confusing pick up spot I had her in my car and was headed for home. Casually I rubbed up and down her meaty thighs feeling the heat grow betwixt them. Once we parked and got inside she was more then willing to jump right into it. Heading upstairs and plopped down on my loveseat like she was told, awaiting further instructions. I grabbed the sex bag and headed upstairs ready to give it my all.

Certain giveaways tell you whether a person does this a lot. Key phrases get used and certain questions get asked typically. Your goal of an encounter is to not only worry about your comfort, but also the comfort of your partner. A shaved private place could very well indicate she was hoping to hook up today. Razor bumps mean it was spur of the moment. Sexy underwear show that this was pre-planned while granny panties tell a different story all together. No bra or panties would display to me full commitment to getting down while wearing both shows slight hesitance. A special tattoo in a special place can mean the world to some and tell epic tales. This girl had none of that, she was Plain Jane, run-of-the-mill average.

Nevertheless she was willing and she was waiting.

Eager was I to carve out another notch, but I was also very eager to make her satisfied. Big girls seem to be more common in the world of hookups then thin ones. Perhaps because they have reduced confidence or maybe even less opportunities due to preconceived judgments. Personally I prefer a thicker gal, the feeling of ribs on my hands is not a pleasant one as I embrace them. They also seem to bring more to the table then skinny girls. They make that extra effort that makes me truly appreciate them. More cushion for the pushin' in combination with a considerate personality makes for a good time all around.

This particular girl would do none of that. She clearly did not have her heart in it from my view. She wanted to be pleased, and pleased she was. I ate her pussy a good thirty minutes before she tapped out. When asked if she wanted to reciprocate she said yes, giving me the poorest attempt at a handjob I've ever had. From her view the man was supposed to do all the work, his pleasure should be in making her happy. I was happy, just not happy enough. I let her give up on the handjob and took her home. She messaged me later, thanking me and wanting to do it again. I was willing to give her another shot and set up a pickup for that Friday, praying things would be better than they had been at our initial meeting.

That Friday I picked her up and brought her back to my place once more. Her attitude seemed better but once again she wanted my tongue between her legs. I gave in, giving her what I had to offer. My tongue a ballerina on her clit putting on a ballet. She came several times, each time pulling my hair and screaming,"Fuck yes!" That was good enough for me, I wanted more.

The idea of another handjob did not sound amusing to me at all. At this point from the example she had shown before I would have much rather done it myself. To my surprise she did not offer head, but in fact offered her pussy as a sacrifice. Placing it upon the loveseat shaped altar I slid on a rubber and got to it. Her cunt, far from a worn road, offered a nice alternative and I felt happy. She refused to do any work still, unwilling to move or participate any more then was absolutely necessary. A compromise I was willing to accept. I felt myself about to explode so I asked her where I should finish. Her answer was in the condom. Not the answer I wanted but the answer I accepted.

I picked up the pace, pushing myself over the edge to a nice orgasm. My condom swelled with my baby batter, her cunt squeezing around me wishing I had came inside. This girl did not know how to make a man happy. I had my notch though, I never needed to see her again if I did not want too. We cleaned up and I drove her home, knowing full well she was going to message me later wanting more. Sure enough *ding* she did.

We talked for awhile that night about what each of us wanted out of this. I'm a sensible man and understand certain individuals are not comfortable with all things. This is an easy work around as eventually we could find common ground. After some long negotiations we were agreed, she would come over that next Tuesday and we would try again. If all went well she would leave happy and so would I. The plan was to bring her over and eat her out for a third time. After that, we would fuck, and if I managed not to bust inside her while wearing a condom I would be rewarded with her mouth waiting to swallow my seed.

She agreed to let me blow inside her mouth as long as she had a drink nearby to get it out as quickly as possible. She did not like the taste, sight, or smell of cum. Here is a life lesson for the ladies out there, if this is also your situation LIE. Men like to be appreciated and it is a massive turn on to see a woman devour his seed. Roll it around in your mouth and get it all over your tongue. Your man will be very grateful I can guarantee it.

I could have given up right then and there but I was hopeful I could make things better. To me, she was more than attractive enough to keep my interest. Her attitude was the only thing that needed a small tweak to keep things going. If I could keep her as a once in the while thing or even a once a month thing I could have been happy. Something to float me through in the dry times. An emergency use pussy if you will.

Intent on making her my backup meant giving her the time of her life on our third meeting. I wanted to show her that if she was willing to go the extra mile for me I would do the same for her. When I picked her up this time she was wearing a long navy blue skirt and a white blouse. Truly she looked stunning as I felt her up on the ride over. Feeling up her leg I worked my way to her pussy. She still wore underwear but this time, they were already soaked through by the time I felt her mound. She was ready for me, but I wanted to tease her as long as I could to make her cum as hard as possible.

Things moved as slow as she would let them. I kissed every inch of her body, paying special attention to her neck. The pecks I gave made her hot under the collar for sure. My hands played with her breasts as I eagerly lapped at her nipples. She slid down her panties, and you could hear them hit the linoleum floor they were so wet. Soon after her skirt, blouse, and bra followed suit. She squirmed as over and over I dodged her sopping wet cunt. I had her right where I wanted her.

My calloused hands made quick work of her. No gloves this time, she was so wet that friction would not be an issue. Her pussy practically sucked the skin off my hand trying to pull it in. Her love muscle spasmed uncontrollably as I finally entered. A small squirt came out and ran down my arm as I held my position. She was hyper sensitive and ready to explode. A powder keg just waiting for a lone spark to set her off.

Her clit, the size of a jellybean, was gonna be my main focus. I was fully on top of her, her nipple in my mouth as I started to open and close my hand with two fingers inside her cunt. With every squeeze she moaned as I put pressure on her clit and g-spot at the same time. I felt her starting to gush but I did not change pace. I kept it steady, feeling her cunt shoot out all over the loveseat. I kept squeezing, pumping her cunt dry. Her legs wrapped around me pulling me even closer. Her breath was hot on my neck and I could feel my now erect cock pressing hard into her leg, clearly visible through my sweatpants.

She was still cumming, squirting with every forceful squeeze. When she started to beg.
" I want you inside me. Please put it inside me." She begged as she gasped for breath. Her arms locked tight around my wrist while she came again.

I backed off, soaking wet halfway up my forearm. I donned a condom and bent her over the loveseat. This time she seemed to act a little different. She rocked back against me, forced me deeper inside of her snatch. I was as deep as I could get and things felt amazing. I pounded her good and thorough and was getting ready to ejaculate. She leaned back and what she said next caught me off guard.
" I want you to cum inside me." She said, squeezing her tits while she said it.
" You want me to take the condom off?" I asked, somewhat confused.
" No leave it on, just cum inside, I can give you head next time. Okay?"

I slowed down to a stop. This bitch was trying to pull a fast one. After all I had done for her, going the extra mile to make sure every need she could possibly have would be satisfied, she still tried dodging the blowjob. Had I known she was going to say that I would never have brought her over that final time. What a moment ago was hopeful optimism of a brighter future was now fear and anger from memories past. I had been lead on and lied to before and was not about to let that happen again.

    I withdrew from her, sliding off the condom and letting it hit the floor. She turned around and squeezed my cock with her hands.
    " Do I really have to?" She asked
    " If you want to see me again, yes. A deal's a deal." I replied.
    Reluctantly and with no shortage of pouting she agreed. I sat on the couch and prepared to do what was going to happen two minutes prior. Had she not brought it up I would have blown inside her for sure, blissfully unaware of my missed opportunity. Her trying to sneak her way out of it was her downfall. That blunder showed me who she really was. Not someone looking to change, but someone looking to take advantage any way she could. I was now ready to unload every last drop into her without regret.

    My plan I had in my head originally was to only shoot once inside her mouth and shoot the rest over her face. A quick towel job and the evidence would be long gone. Now that idea had gone out the window. There had been a small improvement on her participation percentage this time so I decided to do what was in my power to get as much of it down her throat as possible. Save her the taste and hopefully make it a little less severe. Like it or not the tidal wave was coming, best not be near where she makes landfall.

She bobbed up and down, sucking her little heart out. She was determined to make me finish fast as possible and just get it over with. Her speed and dexterity were admirable. The way she fondled my balls as she sucked me deep brought immense joy to me. Every time I was close to cumming she would change positions not knowing, I wasn't about to tell her. She was edging a man with swollen aching balls. She popped up and looked me in the eyes.
" Can you just cum already? I'm trying to go home." She snapped. Apparently she had plans.

I told her sure and grabbed the sides of her head controlling the speed. In no time at all I was ready to bust. As I felt it oozing out of the tip I forced her the whole way down to the base and erupted down her throat. I held her there as she tried to back off, sending torrents of seed to her stomach. She choked and a bunch shot out her nose all over me. It was disgusting and erotic all at the same time. I let her pop off, coughing like crazy and with each cough a little bit of jizz flew out. She surely smelled and tasted it now. No beverage was strong enough to rid her of my essence for some time.

After cleaning up that natural disaster of a load she threw on her clothes and asked me to take her home. I happily obliged, smiling the whole fucking way at my accomplishment. For some odd reason she never messaged me to hook up again. That did not bother me. The people I want to spend intimate moments with not only want me to make them happy but want to make me happy too. Pleasure is a two way street in my book. Honesty is a necessity. Never tell someone what they want to hear, just because you think that will make them happy. For when the time comes to make good on your promises, you better be ready to deliver.

CHAPTER FOURTEEN
Big Dog

To better understand the complexity of this next story I ask you to examine it with an objective lens. Imagine for just a moment that you are the captain of a pirate ship bound for shore. Your ship, so overloaded with plunder that it would not survive the slightest of downpours. As you make your way for land, you see a ship adrift in the waters and go to investigate. As you approach you notice it reminds you of your own vessel, it is loaded to the brim with treasure just as yours, no crew or captain in sight. Your crew is stretched to the breaking point and there is no way to get both to land. You spy dark clouds on the horizon, knowing you have to make a choice. Do you jump ship and hope the treasure is even higher, do you try and sail both to shore and risk losing it all, or do you stick with your ship? The one that, just moments ago, was more then you ever dreamed you'd posess, a treasure so precious your mind can hardly comprehend it.

Not to sound braggadocious, but the amount of

success I had hunting down virgins, was quite impressive. It was one of my target groups, my bread and butter so to speak. Through countless hours and endless clicks on roughly a dozen sites, I had managed to pop a total of nine cherries since I had started the conquest. Throw in Emily and Scarlet from previous chapters and I was at eleven, I wanted a dozen.

My approach to the notches had changed, no longer was it that mad dash to the finish just to say I was done. Now more then ever I was trying to give each notch meaning. I yearned for the emotional satisfaction as well as the physical. I stopped posting ads for single mothers, lessons on squirting, and general hookup ads. I only had one goal, my twelfth virgin and also, my fortieth notch.

The next several months became an arduous hunt for " the one" . I kept getting offers from those who had little experience, but were not virgins. Unfortunately they were not what I was looking for at the time. I was determined to wait out the dry spell. I knew if I kept hunting, kept setting that hook in the water that someday someone was going to take a bite. I knew I was right, everyday I received hate mail from all of the salty men who were just trying to get their dick sucked. They mocked me, said the worst things under the sun in hopes I would be discouraged. Don't hate the player, hate the game. June 12th was when she finally answered my ad having been looking at it for several weeks. She had tossed the idea over in her mind that long and finally, she was willing to try.

She was the farthest away of all my hookups, driving over an hour to come meet me. She was exactly what I was hoping to find, almost a carbon copy of Monica but a virgin. Her name was Sally, she was less then a week out of high school and wanted my services. For her, graduating a virgin was not a choice. She was a really late bloomer, not hitting puberty until late junior year. She had received attention once she finally blossomed but knew they were just after her body now. She was the same girl she was a year before, just without her amazing tits and bubble butt. Her skin the shade of cocoa powder and her hair, naturally black was dyed dirty blonde. She truly looked incredible.

I had gotten lucky before with the mermaid, but this, this was far greater. More then I expected and twice what I deserved. She had driven over willing to lose her innocence to me, a self claimed expert in the field. Her hormones and imagination ran wild as I brought her in. Her breathing sounded panicked. Definitely nervous but willing. Slowly I gave her a firm hug.

"Everything is going to be okay, you're in good hands", I whispered as I held her close. I felt her begin to relax a bit. She was going to be just fine.

Due to her fear I decided the living room was the best place to do this. I had an ottoman, large enough to support her and easy enough to cover with a towel. Slowly she shed the layers, and slowly my cock began to rise. We had discussed through emails what the goal of today was. All she wanted was to lose her cherry, not be made love to, not fucked raw, just wanted to no longer be a virgin. She was shy, but deep inside I knew she was a wild one. Her id, suppressed by her superego, was just waiting to be brought front and center. Inside I knew she yearned to turn from innocent schoolgirl to a cum drunk cockwhore. Her teacher's special cum-dumpster.

As her sun dress hit the floor it revealed her powder blue panties. There was a huge wet spot I could see from several feet away. She was definitely ready for me, and as I watched her slide those panties down I was definitely ready for her. Her freshly shaved mound greeted me like an old friend. A cheerful smile across the lips. I had her assume the position and spread her wide to check out what I was working with. You may not know this, but there is more then one type of hymen and once you know which one you're working with it makes it much easier to make a conscious plan to break it as pain free as possible.

Sadly for her, there was no way to break this one without pain. She was soaking wet, lubrication was not the issue. The issue was her hymen, it was septate. Imagine for a second a small circle, just big enough to get your pinky through if you're lucky. That would be known as a microperforate hymen and was most common in the girls that honored me with that task. Hers was septate, so imagine that small hole with a line going down the center cutting it in two. This was gonna require surgical like precision. Ever so slowly I slid on the condom knowing this was gonna hurt her a lot more then it was gonna hurt me. She was on all fours, breathing deep to stay calm.

"Now because of the type of hymen you have this is going to hurt a bit, only for a short while and then you'll be good.Undersand"? She nodded, it was time.

Gently I prodded her, praying that the band running through the middle would give way. The tension was a hair too loose on it and instead of tearing I was going up one side. She whimpered as I slid in, using my cock alone to try and tear it, only upon reaching the base of my cock did it rip. A small scream escaped her as I felt her pussy clench around me. I was frozen, unable to move while her body tried to react to mine. The sensations were so strong even one wiggle and I would have fell over the edge and finished right then and there.

Thirty seconds later I began to slowly slide in and out. Every thrust brought her farther from pain and closer to pleasure. Her breaths still slow and shaky as over and over again I found myself lightly bouncing off her cervix. Her body had never felt anything like this before and I saw her tensing up, I knew she was close to orgasm. I sped up, still far from lightning speed but a steady pounding now. She forced her ass against me, a low moan escaped her as I felt her cunt spasming uncontrollably. Too much for me to handle I held her close, pushing the limits of what that condom could handle. My natural instincts telling my body to release everything it had. I panicked as I felt a warm sensation run down my balls. I thought the condom had failed but luckily, it was only a few drops of the blood that escaped her. Slowly I withdrew and put the towel in my place, intent on catching any remaining spillage.

I walked to the kitchen, sliding my condom off and throwing it in the trash, leaving Sally alone to ease back down to earth. When I returned she was sitting on the couch now, still shaky in breath, with what looked like tears in her eyes.
"Is everything okay" I asked.
"I'm sitting on a strangers couch with blood coming out of my vagina, do I look okay???" Sally shot back
"You look beautiful. Don't worry, the hard part is over now. You only need to break it once, you won't hurt or bleed again." I replied
"Will I ever see you again, now that I'm not a virgin?" She asked with a look of sadness in her eyes.
"If you're willing to come back, I will see you as often as you like. My name's Rick by the way, Rick Labour."

With that she smiled and threw her sun dress back on. She slowly slid up those powder blue panties and let them rest against her still sore pussy. I walked her to the door. Before she left she turned around, looking down at my still swollen member still covered partially in my seed. I had not gotten dressed for I was going to hop in the shower after she left. She reached out, dancing her finger around the head and stealing the last drop of cum that had leaked out. She brought the finger to her mouth and slowly licked it clean.
" See you soon," she said, as she left. This girl was

gonna be a fucking keeper.

We messaged each other constantly, her mind racing with all of the things she wanted to try. My experience was a well she wanted to draw from. Three days later she wanted to come over again and luck had it I was free. She was a blank slate that wanted filled in every sense of the word. Super submissive and willing to try anything. I told her this time, I wanted to teach her how to squirt. Her orders were simple, on the drive over I wanted her to play with herself at every red light. By the time she arrived I would be ready to finish her off.

I was eagerly awaiting her arrival, when the doorbell rang I leapt from my seat and hurriedly made my way to the door. It was Sally, standing there in all her glory. As I invited her in I noticed she was wearing the same dress as the last time. Memories came rushing back as I shut the door, staring at her figure brought the primal urges back.
"I've got a surprise for you!" she said excitedly as we walked to the center of the room and kicked off her shoes.
"What's the surprise?" I asked. With that her dress hit the floor revealing sexy white lace lingerie. My heart thundered in my chest as I looked her over. The contrast of her rich dark skin against the white fabric was too arousing. I felt my pants grow tight around me, the fabric struggling to contain my erection.

She got on her knees in front of the couch and tapped the cushion gesturing me to sit down. I shed my pants and sat down. My cock eagerly twitching just a foot from her face. Slowly she ran her fingers up and down my shaft. She may have been the one who looked like chocolate but I was the one melting as she licked me from base to head. A single drop escaped me which she quickly removed. Leaning back and licking her lips right after.

"You tasted so good last time I thought I would come back for more." She said, sliding her hand up and down my shaft.

"Are you sure you can handle it, there might be a lot." I replied with a confident smile .

"We will have to wait and see." She said smirking at me and taking me in her warm mouth. Her lips hot as cocoa, her tongue like warm honey.

She wanted to suck me dry and with that outfit on there wasn't much I could do to stop her. Her tits were perfectly cradled and popping in and out of view. Her supple ass wiggled behind her as she went to town on me. The pressure was building, I warned her she would have a mouthful soon. She sped up, flicking her tongue back and forth as she coaxed my balls to empty between her teeth. It was a two gulper but she took it like a champ. As the soul gently returned to my body, I felt obliged to return the favor.

I stood her up and removed her stylish undergarments. I played with one tit, sucked on the other. My other hand slid to her slit and found its way to her clit. One brush and she shivered. She was just as ready as she had been at our first meeting, her cunt eagerly awaited my touch. I laid down a towel, having a good inclination that I would be successful and that this girl would be a squirter.

My tongue made its way in, she started to moan as I lapped up the sweet nectar that was her cuntwater. I reached up inside her and felt her g-spot. Her patch was rugged and swollen to capacity. Her young sex yearning to release if given the chance. I began to rake, feeling her muscles tighten around my hand as she came. I continued on , fighting in hand to gland combat until finally, she started to squirt. Her hot juices shooting down my arm as her legs locked around me. This girl was kinky, so I wanted to take this one step further. I led her to the mudroom .

In my home there is a mudroom that links to the living room, the front door opens and in front of it stands a tinted glass door. You can see out but no one can see in. We were both naked as I opened the door, her eyes as wide as dinner plates as I told her what to do next. I told her to stand there in front of me and put her hands on the frame. I wanted to make her squirt as she watched the outside world go by. Cars driving, people walking by and chatting. Some out on their porch reading the paper.

I got to work and soon enough she started squirting, spilling herself all over the tile floor below. My hands manipulated her cunt , hitting all the right buttons over and over to make her blow. I reached inside the living room and grabbed a condom. Never have I ever gotten one on as fast as I got right back in there, this time finding her spot with my rock hard cock rather then my hand. We would fuck, she would empty herself all over the floor, I would give her thirty seconds to rest and the cycle would begin anew. What once were chirps had turned to moans, what were moans were now yelps. Luckily no one was within view of the door so we were fine. It was no longer a choice, I needed to cum.

She was getting sore and I could take the pressure no longer. I slammed good and hard into her as I approached the edge, one final clench and I was going to blow. She was starting to cum too as I noticed the mailman making his way to my porch.

I came hard, grunting as I felt her cunt lock around me. I felt myself pulsing as I forced one hand over her mouth and the other I used to grab the door handle. The mailman stood there just inches away from our pulsing genitals as he put the mail in the box. A small package had apparently arrived for us today. He grabbed for the door handle as I held it with the force of god. When it did not yield he simply laid it at the door and knocked twice before walking away. Fucking hell that was fun.

We laid the towel over the waterlogged mudroom floor and sat down to rest. Both of us excited and aroused by our risk taking. Today she put her underwear in her purse, her cunt too sensitive to be touched. A gentle hug was our parting contact as she made her way back out to the world. Before hopping in the shower I decided to pour myself a celebratory drink. I am a rum guy, love my aged dark rum on ice.

Minimum two fingers, sometimes three.

My phone buzzed as I plopped back down. It is Sally sending me all these messages.
"Hey I just wanted to let you know your neighbor heard us"
"I hope this does not make things awkward for you around your neighborhood"
"I had an amazing time, can't wait to see you again !"

I shot back a series of questions to try and find out who actually heard us. I have neighbors on both the left, and the right. Either would be a little awkward to talk to. After her long drive home she saw my messages and wrote back.
"It was neither of them , It was a black man across the street." An answer I was not expecting. He was close to sixty feet from my front door. Had we really been that loud?

My heart sunk, no one in the neighborhood knew about our lifestyle. We try and keep it a secret to avoid all of the awkward questions, judgments, and of course solicitations. I tossed the idea over in my mind, the idea of him spreading the news of what happened. He was a huge gossip and everyone knew it. If he was honest about what had happened, my street cred would have improved highly with the ladies. Someone who can lay the pipe like that may even get an offer or two from the neighborhood trollops.

Several days had passed when I had my encounter

with the witness. Sitting on his porch he beckoned me over. This guy was far from an honest man like me. He was not only a dealer of drugs, but he was trying to broaden his horizons by becoming a pimp as well. A true entrepreneur in his own right. The conversation went from a sort of congratulations to blackmail. He argued his silence had value.

I looked him dead in the eye and said, " Pretty sure she knows bud, we got a three way planned for tomorrow."

He was defeated but could not help but smile. As I made my way to the car I heard him yell," Alright big dog, you do you!"

With that short interaction I got confidence like I never had before. No longer did I have fear of rejection from my lifestyle. I became determined to throw myself out there and see their reactions. Most were positive, but one was a call to a higher power. We were a half dozen misfit warehouse workers but among us was a man of great faith, let's call him Mr.G. He had been through a layoff and a serious health issue but his faith remained strong. He was the only one who cared for not only my worldly happiness but also my eternal one. His kind words planted a mustard seed of faith which took years to sprout, but only that moment to plant.

That next morning I was filled with anxiety and anticipation. I wasn't lying when I told my neighbor about the three way. She was coming at eleven and I had to be prepared to give the fuck of my life. Never had I ever had two been with two women that made my heart flutter. I prayed I could handle what was about to go down.

It was ten thirty when I send Monica to the basement while I got the living room ready. The plan was simple and there was no need or time for a test run. Once Sally arrived I was to get her all hot and bothered, then call up Monica to join us. I got a text saying she was here and walking up the block. I raced to meet her at the door. As I opened it she was there, same dress as the past two times. Don't fix what ain't broken right? As I let her in I saw my neighbor sitting on his porch, a slight look of disbelief on his face. He could see Monica's car there and knew she was home.

Sally was already hot and bothered when she arrived. Over our texts she said she was excited that she was getting to meet Monica for the first time. Deep down I think Sally wanted to be in her spot but she would never say it. The way she looked at me was with lust with just a splash of love. The way I had looked at Monica from the first time I saw her. As I watched Sally strip, once again revealing that outfit that could make your toes curl, I yelled down the stairs.
"Honey can you come up here and help us for a minute?" and with that she began to climb up, ready to ravish both of us.

As she entered the room my heart fluttered from the sight of her. She was nude, her massive breasts swinging as she walked towards us. An angel in human form. She motioned for me to sit and knelt down by my right knee, pointing Sally my left. My mouth was dry, unable to speak as they tag teamed little Rick. Their tongues battled as they tried to French kiss each other around my cock. Each one showing their skills, wanting to be the one to make me erupt. They were treating this like a competition but I was the real winner. As I felt myself get close to giving them both a bath with my hot baby batter I motioned Monica to the seat next to me. Her turn.

I grabbed Sally by the hair and guided her to Monica's cunt. The sight was too much, I had to look away as I slid a condom on. The moans and groans drove me to the breaking point as I ever so gracefully slid inside Sally. Her tongue did not miss a beat as I pounded her tight cunt, forcing myself not to cum inside. Monica looked down, saw the expressions I was making, and gave me a look. The look of , " That is my cum sir, you better switch us up if you're about to nut." As much as I wanted to hold off longer I just could not, I told Sally and Monica to switch places. All I did was lean back and slide off the condom, now ready to flood Monica's womb.

Monica was even tighter and hotter then Sally had been. No man could have lasted long in a position like this. Your dick is balls deep in your fiancee, your fiancee's face is buried deep in your side piece's meat pocket, and your side piece is staring into your soul while she gently bites her bottom lip. She watches you explode inside your soon to be wife and follows your example by water boarding her with her juicy muff. All three orgasm as your train of sexual satisfaction gently pulls into the station. Exhausted, you lay down on the ground, your last bit of energy used to pull Monica down with you, exposing the massive creampie you left behind. Monica sticks her hand down, gets some of my cum on her hand and brings it to her face. Laps it up like its candy. Not to be outdone, Sally joins us on the floor and her face finds its way to Monica's cum-flooded fuck-tunnel. She proceeds to suck out every drop she can. We lay there, fully satisfied.

Time never stops and we did have other plans for the day. As I shakily got up and sat on the couch Monica also got up.
"I'm going to go upstairs and get a shower, after that we can go. It was nice meeting you Sally."
"Nice meeting you, too." Sally replied as we both watched Monica's ass bounce as she climbed the stairs. I could feel myself getting hard again.
"Hey I have another surprise for you, but you need to close your eyes." She said with a grin ear to ear. We heard the water of the shower kick on.
"Fair enough." I replied and closed my eyes. Before I could tell her to stop I was the whole way inside her. Raw.

"What the fuck do you think you're doing???" I whispered.
"I have plan B inside my bag, I will take it when I get to my car. I'm not leaving without your cum inside me." With that she began to ride me. Her hips rocking

and her tight cunt squeezing me for dear life. Harder and harder she bounced until I could take it no longer. I exploded inside her and as I did she let out a whimper. Her pussy tugged at me wanting everything I had in the tank. I ran it dry.

Before getting off of me she leaned in close. She kissed me slowly and said thank you as she pulled away. She dressed herself, pulling up those white lace panties and still leaking my load. As she left she said not a word, only ruffled my hair as she passed by shutting the door behind her. What the fuck had just happened? This kinky bitch was trying to win me over and I cannot say she isn't succeeding. Could it be possible I loved her back? What would that mean for Monica and I ?

I sat there exhausted, confused, and worried. I had just had the best sex of my life with the two greatest women I had ever been inside. Both wanted me as more then a lover and I had to make a choice. I sat there and really thought about how I felt. Things had not changed since I met Sally. I still loved Monica and knew she was my soulmate. I wanted to marry her and grow old together. My decision was made before Sally came into my life, you can only have one soulmate and Monica was mine.

Polyamorous relationships are just not my style. Had this happened hundreds of years ago we definitely would have formed a happy harem. As far as modern day goes, Sally was just a crush and would in no way replace what I currently had. I could have included more short stories about Sally and I. Could have written a small book about her alone if I am being honest. Sadly this chapter has gone on long enough.

Over the next month I saw Sally about a half dozen times, each time having a different experience. We tried anal, bdsm, roleplay, you name it. I taught her what I could with the time we had left to share. She was going off to college soon and needed to be prepared. When she arrived she was super shy and very nervous but when I was done with her the confidence she had could dominate a room. Her body, once something she was ashamed of, was now her greatest aid in seduction.

The end of summer came and I had to bid farewell. She was off to a school halfway across the country and odds were she wasn't coming back. We texted back and forth up until she found a boyfriend on campus. Once she found someone I told her we had to break it off. I did not want some drunken text from me to ruin a possibility of her finding her soul mate. We said our farewells and I blocked her number and deleted every email. That was the hardest thing, not knowing how she was doing even a second after I blocked her. I truly hope she has found all the happiness in the world.

I had inspected the ship and found it wanting. Although the treasure was a grand one, it was in no way worth abandoning my own for. My treasure was priceless, my bounty abundant. I was not meant to be captain of this ghost ship that was set adrift. Her booty was more then I could handle so I cast off and made my way for sure. Looking back and seeing clouds in the distance I could only hope someone else would be lucky enough to find her. A captain even more worthy then I to take the helm. I sleep soundly at night knowing that although I was not meant to be captain, I was one hell of a first mate.

CHAPTER FIFTEEN
Cancer

The mere mention of the word conjures up emotions in most. Nowadays you would be hard-pressed to find someone who has not been impacted in some way, shape, or form by its evil. Half my family has had it, most didn't make it through. They suffered up until their dying breath. Cancer strips everything from you, it changes you and not for the better. Those unfortunate enough to be diagnosed need all the love they can get. Let not the condition define them, allow the content of their character to show who they really are.

To this day I have never said no to anyone based solely on their physical attractiveness. Some would say that is low standards but I see that as having an open mind. Your size and appearance mean a lot less to me then your personality. Open honest communication with a dash of sincerity is all I am looking for in a good friend. True beauty lies within, your body is just a vessel to carry out your worldly desires.

I found Michelle on a dating site several years back. She looked normal, a typical suburban mom with a Karen hair-do. She had a decent set of tits which drew your eyes in. God was she thin. Nowhere on her body could you pinch an inch. Her pale skin made her ruby red lipstick make you forget everything else about her face.

We were two of a kind in a way, both of us were in "complicated" relationships. While Monica and I were in an open relationship, Michelle was in a much more interesting kind of setup. She was a submissive who was "owned" by a Dom who was kind enough to let her pick who else she could play with. There was an approval process where I had to say why I wanted to borrow her and what my intentions were. I was truthful and with only a few minutes of thinking and a picture of me, he said I was good to go. He told me the main reason I got approved is because my dimples were just so gosh darn cute.

Still even after winning approval from her Dom I was not much closer to being with her. She was highly unsure of herself and extremely self conscious of her appearance. Afraid that once I saw her in person I would be disgusted by her and run off. After many assurances of my dedication to the task, she dropped the bombshell that the reason she was so thin was because she had breast cancer. Her bust was not her own, a double mastectomy took her twins away and these were just implants. It was going to take more then that to scare me off.

It was kind of nice having a mature woman for once. No need to sneak out *and* she was able to drive herself over. Two things that made me like her already. We set up a time when both of our partners would be at work. She arrived fashionably late but with good reason. Her figure was caped in full gothic regalia. Dressed to the nines as a queen of the night with a full length black lace skirt leading down to combat boots. Her chest highly accentuated by a tightly drawn Victorian style corset. She even did her hair, what was in her profile picture a blonde Karen style cut was now a set of black pony tails. For reference I do live in a very bad neighborhood, one which she stood out like a sore thumb. Quickly I invited her in to get better acquainted.

This notch was more to me then just sex. This was a human being who was going through unimaginable suffering in life and I was a small glimpse of light in the darkness. To rush this would be throwing a genuine opportunity at human kindness down the drain. She had reduced her own self worth to one of being a mans sexual property. Perhaps I could be a turning point in her life, maybe even a new chapter.

Even though she was sexual property, her needs had not been met in a long time. She wanted for nothing on the dark side of sex. She had a man willing to do whatever sick twisted thing she could come up with. I was the light to balance out the dark. A gentle lover is what she was truly longing for. She yearned to trade in the chokes for gentle strokes.

There is no sexy way to take off a corset. If there is I have no clue what witchcraft you speak of. For me, it was like untying a sexy pair of sneakers. I spent a few minutes untying it before it finally hit the floor. We had not made it far, just inside my living room when we started to undress her. I explored her figure, sliding my hands up her sides . So thin I could feel her ribs as I slid up to her breasts. They were definitely different.

Cool to the touch and firmer then any breasts I had ever grabbed. They were nice, the only difference from normal at a distance was a small scar under each one where the incision was. Gently I kissed her neck as my hands went lower. Dragging my fingers around her narrow waist just under her waistband. I did not feel any underwear underneath. She let out a gasp as the skirt hit the floor.
"What are you going to do to me?" Michelle asked, a sense of excitement in her voice.
"I'm going to worship your body like a temple." I replied and with that I took her by the hand.

Her boots clacked as she followed me around the couch to her awaiting spot. Michelle was a true sub, and for the time we were together I was in charge of her. The only things I could not make her do was what was on a very short list her Dom had sent. If it was not on the list, she would obey. Ever the obedient servant. Willing to suck a strangers cock dry at a moments notice in order to please. Never expecting praise, nor reward for her deeds.

Initially it was difficult to be accepted as a human being with feelings. I knew she wanted to serve, so I sat down on the couch and spread my legs. My order was direct and succinct.
"Suck me dry Michelle, suck me dry."

Without missing a beat she fell to her knees and started worshiping my cock. Her frail body leaned in against my thighs. She was too small to block my view of her cunt. Her whole body, minus her head, was hairless. A side effect that made her look much younger then she was. I had never seen a woman mid thirties that smooth. Her swirling vortex of a tongue and careful tossing of my balls had me on the edge of release. I avoided the urge to clench, for doing so would have splattered the back of her throat. Instead I let her suck it drop by drop from my hose.

She leaned back on her feet, a sense of pride across her face as my pressure stabilized.
"That was very good Michelle, your looks are only surpassed by your oral skills." I said as her cheeks began to blush.
"What do you want me to do next?" She asked, wearing the innocent face of someone who didn't just suck a cock.
"We are going to switch spots now, it's your turn." I replied.
"I get a turn? Oh… okay, sure." She said as she stood up, utterly shocked at my kindness.

I took my time, maybe too much time. Explored every sensitive area on that womans body. Her breasts were all day suckers waiting to be devoured. Her thighs, so soft and tender against my cheek. Too long had she been ignored and neglected. I could feel her fingernails bury themselves in my skull as I made every lick count. Her hairless cunt, void of flavor, the ultimate dish. Forcefully I licked every angle I could of her clit. Her moans and wails could be heard through the walls by the neighbors I'm sure. She shivered and shook as finally her resistance gave way. Her sex tapped out and convulsed like crazy as she came for the first time in years.

As her panting slowed I dove in again, and no sooner had I gotten to full speed when she came again. Harder this time. This woman was in my home, fully willing to do anything I asked within reason. My penis had recovered and was hungry for more. Her hairless cunt was calling my name. I sat down beside her, condom in hand. Unwrapping it and sliding it down my shaft sent her a clear message - we are far from done.
"Go behind the couch and lean over it, I will meet you there." I ordered. She obeyed.

Her fuckhole was lively and incredibly grateful for my arrival. From the second I began to slide in it began to react. Her thin frame offered no buffer for me to bounce off of. I was going to pound her all the way to the base. Pumping in and out like a machinegun brought me close to finishing in just a few minutes. She was getting dicked down like a ragdoll when I felt her gush. You could hear her squirting, the droplets splashing as they hit the floor. I could take it no longer as I bucked hard, driving myself in deep as I felt myself release. I was kind of bummed that I had to wear a condom. That would have felt amazing in the raw.

Over the next twenty minutes I tried my best to help her get redressed. She was nearly as composed as when she had arrived. Except instead of a graceful stride it was a jelly leg cowboy strut back to the car. She was exhausted and needed to rest. I said goodbye and got a, "thank you sir," in return as she left. I wasn't sure if I would ever see her again, but once her Dom caught wind of what I had done to her, he insisted I see her at least one more time. Excellent.

The next time she came over I told her to be more modest, she begrudgingly accepted and showed up in some black slacks and a bright white blouse. It had only been a week since I had seen her but it appeared she had her hair done yet again. She was back to the Karen cut and had redyed it blond. Not my favorite style but it gave her the appearance of a sexy school teacher or maybe the manager at some random store. It was not her hair I was after, it was her broken spirit.

That day was not going to be as vanilla as last time. Her Dom had given her orders to tell me what I was to do. He wanted a full report after we were done on how I did. I never had to get a report card for sex before. She let me know she was going to be loud if I made her squirt again. The living room was no longer a safe option, we went down to the basement.

Down there the sound would hopefully be muffled by the floor above. I made quick work of removing her clothes this time. Her pants and blouse hit the floor within seconds. This time she had worn panties in a bright shade of yellow. A light wet spot could be seen in her front where the fabric clung to her. I slid them down to her ankles and off her feet. Slowly I folded them up and pressed them firmly into her mouth. No one was going to hear her.

I sat her on a bench I had made with two drywall buckets and some thick boards. Her tiny frame did not even stick out past the sides as she lay down, ready to try and handle all I had to offer. She had no idea what that meant.

It began with licking and then went to sucking her already swollen clitoris. My finger was at a crawl when she first started to cum. Her g-spot received a gentle massage, at least at first. Over and over I repeated this process, each time bringing her just over climax to have the smallest squirt possible. My hands although talented, were not my greatest weapon. Ole Reliable lay at my feet. Still inside his bag, ready to unleash hell.

As I grabbed my toy ready to penetrate her I looked up to see her face. An expression of being drunk on life and fear was across her face. As I slid it inside her she knew everything was going to be okay, more then okay. As it thundered in and out she began to unleash the downpour. Her hands squeezing desperately into the hardwood of the bench. Her pelvis shaking as over and over again her cunt erupts. Ten. Fifteen. Twenty. I refuse to stop until she does. Twenty three was her magic number. My arms were sore as I held it in her. Her fuckhole unable to pump anymore fuck-water out from within her. She would be too sore to fuck today, I would have to settle for more head. After her panting subsided her feeble frame went on the ground, her panties falling to the floor onto shiny concrete.

Taking the position on the bench was easy, holding my cock slop in my body was hard. She seemed determined to empty me at record speed. Her mouth gliding up and down my shaft at record pace. I ground my teeth and grunted as everything in my body flew into her mouth. No longer a babbling brook but a whitewater rapid of semen. She coughed as she tried to take it all in one gulp. She looked up at me and something wasn't right. I noticed her hair was kind of off center, thats when I realized it was a wig.

She was looking up at me, blissfully unaware as she thanked me for my fluids and the pleasure she had received. I know its rude to stare but I simply could not help myself and got caught staring. She tried to fix it when she realized it was off. Tears were in the corners of her eyes.

I stood up and pulled her up too. She was sobbing, ashamed of her own body. No one should ever feel like that.
"Hey," I said as I put my hands on her head, she reached up and put her hands on mine as I slowly

pulled off her wig revealing that her head was also completely bald.

"Next time take it off, I like you more this way," I said as I put a tender kiss upon her lips.

She broke down in tears and hugged me. I could feel her emotions flowing out of her eyes and running down my chest. I wish I could say that it ended there in some romantic movie style way, but it just did not. She was in my eyes attractive and holding me tightly. Her overworked organ radiating heat upon mine. I felt myself swell as another one filled the chamber. She looked down, feeling it ever so gently bump against her swollen sex. She reached down and slowly rubbed my head against her opening. Her love tunnel was rubbed raw, there was no way I would be able to fuck the front, but her ass was untouched. The only hole I had not yet explored.

Shit was getting freaky, she agreed to anal and after I had donned a condom I made my way inside her tight little asshole. My balls swung and slapped her raw lips with every insertion. Closer and closer I came to blowing what little seed I had left. Michelle had done a decent job emptying me and this was all the gas I had left in the tank. The little light was on that said, "get fuel soon". It was blinking.

She had not put the wig back on and I could imagine nothing better the giving her a facial. I couldn't get it in her hair if there was none. The plan was to pray and spray. Her hole was upset I pulled out so soon, it wanted beaten senseless like its buddy in the front. I was not man enough to ruin all three holes in one sitting. A man needs some cookies and a juice box for fuck's sake. Some recovery time to refill. Ericka's hole had me right where it wanted me, squeezing tightly intent on getting every drop out of me it could. She was a master, a true ass-assin in her own right.

I slid off the condom and she took the position in front of me. Accepting of her fate as he eyes closed and she stuck out her tongue. I closed my eyes, the intensity too much as I blasted what little baby batter remained in my poor balls. It went everywhere. Over her eyelids, the nose, the forehead, and even a drop or two on her tongue. Ever the obedient servant she did not ask for a rag, she rubbed it in. She smeared my cock cologne all over herself. Truly a cum-slut in her own right. I left her to clean herself up while I went upstairs and put on fresh clothes. As she came upstairs I arose long enough to give her a good long hug. She kissed me on the cheek, the strong odor of my brew wafting off of her as she did so.

A few hours later I got my grade. It was an A+. Hours later she was still too sore to provide for her man. I felt a sense of accomplishment and pride as I sat there waiting for dinner. Monica was baking a lasagna and the fragrance was exquisite. She had gone down to the basement to smoke when I heard her yell.

"Honey who's panties are these and why are they in my fucking spot?" she yelled.

Michelle had apparently planted her panties so Monica would find them. Was she trying to get me in trouble? Break us up? Either way bad… bad girl.

I tossed over the thought of it being an accident for a while but there was no way in hell it was. Panties don't just fly across the room when they are soaking wet and land on a chair. She had planted them, she needed to be punished.

Michelle was invited over again, this time her man had given me free range to do whatever my heart desired. The plan was to get one more fuck in, a good hate fuck, and then send her packing. Once I got her inside we found our way to the basement again. This time the bench was moved, even farther away to over by the tool bench. I ordered her to suck me off and this time I wanted her to hold my cum in her mouth. Slowly she worked her magic and sure enough I had her cheeks fully filled. I told her to get up and lay on my lap. She was confused but obeyed.

As she lay across my lap my hand violently smacked her ass. A muffled shriek escaped her as my hand made contact. When I moved it away you could see the outlines of all my fingers. She was breathing rapidly, unsure of what was going on. That was when I reached over and grabbed up a rolled up extension cord I had on the work bench, maybe six feet in length, but pretty thick.
"You were a very bad girl Michelle," I said lightly slapping her with the cord. Her ass wiggled with excitement.
"Bad girls get whipped Michelle," I said, smacking her firmly, the wiggling stopped.

"No one tries to fuck up my relationship, no one!" With that I brought the cord down hard. It was so hard it fell from my hand. She screamed, my massive load flying out of her mouth all over her chin and onto the floor. She jumped to her feet clutching her now violated rear end and breathed in sharply. That was enough torture, now to get my nut.

I forced her to double over the bench, exposing her juicy cunt. As tempted as I was to go in raw I would never violate someone like that. Swiftly I slid on a condom and thrust inside. Her juices running down my thighs as made her my bitch. No longer was this about her experiencing the joys of what life had to offer, you lose those privileges when you try and fuck me over. I was manhandling her, slamming her tail bone into me. Her cervix became a punching bag for my unbridled penile fury. My rage subsided as I came. Her limp lifeless sex toy she calls a body was of no more use to me.

You feel like a real man when you're doing that to someone, but once its all over those feelings, at least for me, turn into regret. I rarely have happy feelings after I destroy someone like that. She may have had cancer but for me, she *was* a cancer. After she cleaned herself up I told her she could leave. She tried to kiss me but I backed away. Later that night her owner messaged me and I told him the whole story. He agreed it was best I never see her again.

I never did see her after that, and now I never will. Her cancer returned but this time it took her. I like to think that even if it was only for a few days that I made her life a little better so close to the end. Was I sorry for the way I handled it? Nope. I wish I could say I felt sad about the loss but if I am being totally honest I just can't. No one mourns the wicked.

CHAPTER SIXTEEN
I'm at my prime

As the finish line came into view I was renewed with a sense of passion. A chore can become a labor-of-love as the end is in sight. Life was going very well in every way possible. I had started a new career as a truck driver which seemed to be well within my wheelhouse. Monica and I had just begun to plan our dream wedding. Last, but surely not least, I was at notch number forty nine. The next person who was willing to let me inside them would finally end this genital gauntlet once and for all. I was still in an open relationship mind you, but sex became a strictly for pleasure affair after this. My mind ran wild with who would be lucky enough to find me.

The online classifieds had prooven themselves indispensable. By this time I had been running ads for a shade over seven years. I knew all the ins and outs. Every move was like a chess game, highly strategic. The ad had to be written in such a way that it made you think about it long after first glance. Hopefully after tossing it over, you may change your mind and decide to give me a shot. When I finally got a response to an ad I was delighted. We got to talking and as it turns out, she had been seeing my ad for months. She was on the site daily looking for new clientele. The woman was employed by the world's oldest profession: she was an escort.

After explaining to her that I did not pay for sex, she assured me I would not be charged. I guess for the day she was willing to be a non-profit whoreganization. She had responded to an ad in which I had offered to teach women to squirt. Although she was no stranger to the bedroom, not a single man had been willing to do that for her. This did not come as a shock to me. When time becomes a commodity the satisfaction of your partner can easily be left behind. Where some men saw " used goods", I saw opportunity. Who was I to judge? I was far from fresh out of the box myself. The vagina is a muscle, the more it is worked the better it tends to feel.

She was actually pretty befitting of my target audience. She was very clean, concerned about safety, and willing to learn. To catch something or have a baby would mean a loss of much needed income. Her experience was quite tantalizing. The concept of someone who was good enough to get paid for it on a regular basis was appealing. I felt confident knowing at the bare minimum, I would at least be able to finish.

She invited me over to her apartment for the encounter. It was a calm Saturday afternoon in the middle of September. The air was warm so I took the motorcycle. As I parked I could see her leaning out the window looking for me. She was far from ugly. Her curly shoulder length brown hair focused your gaze. Deep chestnut eyes gave you a hard wood. Her breasts were well presented in a revealing top. She would make for a fine notch, truly worthy to be number fifty.

As I climbed the stairs to her apartment I could feel my heart racing. It all hit me at once. The realization that she was real and this was happening. Within the hour I would be cumming and my conquest would be complete. She welcomed me inside, told me to sit down and watch TV with her while her roommate finished getting ready for work. I was tempted to try and negotiate a three way. Perhaps she would join in on the fun? That would have made an epic final battle if she would have said yes. I let that opportunity pass by as she walked out the door. I was more then content with what I still had with me.

As the door closed my host walked to the window to watch her departure. She wanted to see her car drive away to assure we were safe. She needed to make sure we were uninterrupted in our activities. Her elegantly refined figure was bent over at just the right angle. She could look me in the eyes without shoes on. Her long slender legs led up to an ass any man would be happy to hold. I could sit and watch no longer. Her cute butt was a slowly waving target I intended to hit. I approached her from behind and got real close.

"Is she gone yet? Are we in the clear?" I asked as my hands became well acquainted with her ass.

She let out a low gentle moan as I fondled her. Still

she leaned out the window and watched life go by. My hands went between her thighs and gently rubbed her cunt. The teasing while she was in public view was getting her off. I could feel her getting hotter, her blood flow increasing as I continued to grab her by the pussy. The car was long gone, we both knew that. The kinkiness of the act made us want to keep on going. My hand pressed firmly into her labia. Her legs shook and firmly closed together.

"I think shes gone now, we can start," she said, unwilling to let my teasing continue.

I moved her over to the couch and had her sit on a towel she had ready. I had my usual bag of tools, intent on using what I could to get the job done in a way that she could still go to work tomorrow. Ole reliable had been left at home for just that reason. Knowing this wasn't her first rodeo saved us a good portion of time. There was no true need for foreplay. This felt like more of a business transaction then a hook-up. I knew her time had monetary value and did not want to waste it by dragging this out longer than it had to be. Not that I was not going to enjoy myself, but the tender kissing and sucking to build tension was a step that could be bypassed for the sake of brevity. I donned my gloves and got to work.

Her sex greeted me like an old friend, happy to see me with a firm grip. She rocked her hips as she felt me enter her, her libido yearning to feel satisfaction. I raked her g-spot like there was no tomorrow. With one finger I forced her to squirt. Her cunt was not used to getting this sort of attention. She started leaking lightly on the towel as I kicked it into high gear. I forced a second finger inside her, her reaction instantaneous. The moans turned into wails as she began to pulse. Squirting over and over again. I held my ground, determined not to yield until she told me to stop or she passed out, whichever came first. I felt her pussy lock around my hand.

"Okay okay okay," she said, panting and grabbing my shoulders. My hand was still imprisoned inside her, feeling her rapid heart rate every time she spasmed. Every attempt at withdrawing was met with another clamp down. She was soaked all the way to the knees. So much for the towel.

When her love dungeon finally released me, the gloves came off and latex went on elsewhere. I knew her cunt would dominate my fully engorged fuckstick. Your organ is a muscle, and by that standard she was a power lifter who just did a line of cocaine. If it locked up my dick the way it locked up on my hand I would be done for. I hoped for the best as I pressed myself deep inside her. Her legs wrapped around me as our hips met. A look of ecstasy covered her face as I found my way deeper and deeper inside her. I wanted to show her what was possible with the right guy so I pulled her legs off my sides and threw them on my shoulders. I squatted just enough to hammer directly on her g-spot. She began to leak once more, her body yielding to my will. Her hot juices flowed over me on their way out. I could not help but shiver as I felt them running down my legs.

This went on for a few cycles, but I was too close

to orgasm to go even one more round. Her bearded clam had a mind of its own and wanted my seed. Her instincts had taken over. Her primal urges of yearning to be bred were coming to the surface. Her nipples fully erect as her breasts giggled with every slam. Her head leaned back and her mouth was wide open, she made every pleasurable sound imaginable. I asked her where I should finish, she said in her mouth. I cautiously withdrew from her box, The condom was swelled at the end. Enough pre-cum had come out to form a bubble. The second I got that condom off she was already at my cock, squeezing the vein filled man meat tightly and sliding her lips onto my tender flesh.

Her silky tongue gently caressed my swollen ham candle the second her lips parted. She was a lover by trade, a true master in her craft. She edged me with such grace and sophistication. Her oral skills were her true talent, and she had no problem showing it off. I looked towards the sky, unable to fight the urge any longer. That serpent between her lips forced an eruption that rivaled a volcano. No less then ten pumps of cum found their way to her tonsils. As I looked down I saw her slowly sliding off. My rod was hypersensitive as her lips were locked around my shaft. She was intent on getting every last drop she had worked for. At the tip she released with a loud pop, looking up at me with a sense of both gratitude and pride.

Truly, I wish that this could have been more than a one-time thing. Sadly, business is business. As we dressed we began to talk and I learned a lot in just a short time. For her, men were not looking to have sex all the time. Most were older men who just wanted to be around a pretty young girl. She was maybe twenty five years old, most of her clients were in their mid fifties. A few of them did want sex, but overall they were just happy to cuddle on the couch and order a pizza. I complimented her talents, letting her know how appreciative I was at how she finished me off. Her response sticks with me to this day.

"Anyone can suck a dick, what you do is true talent. Thank you for teaching me what my body is capable of."

With that I said goodbye and made my way back to my motorcycle. Firing it up, I took one last look at the window. She was there watching me. I noticed her shoulder was moving. That kinky bitch was touching herself as she watched me leave. I started my bike and waved goodbye. She gently blew me a kiss with her free hand. I rode away from there with nothing left to prove to anyone. As the wind ripped through me I was finally free. The bondage of my own self doubts had been broken. I was not some ugly garbage someone had taken pity on, I was a man. A man worthy of love and respect. I was not washed up, I was in my prime. I was proud, and pride always cometh before the fall.

CHAPTER SEVENTEEN
Rock Bottom, or close to it

What comes up surely must come down. My goal for notches had been achieved, with no goal in mind what do I do now? Being a man-whore was my identity, it was all I knew. I had no real hobbies besides trying to put my dick in things. If only I had sat back at the time and reevaluated my options I may have chosen a different path. At the time of this encounter I was blissfully unaware of the executive order that would bring it all crashing down once and for all.

Through the development of my own sexuality over the course of my journey I cared less and less about the physical release and more about the emotional gratification. I wanted to be some sort of karmic force in the universe and right the injustices I saw. Life goes by faster then we want it to, some will inevitably fall behind or not be given the same chances as others.

A woman responded to my ad with the wish to

learn to squirt. Her story was one full of loss, a woman widowed at a young age who had not been with a man in over thirty years. She needed this, maybe more then anyone I had met thus far.

She was full of doubt, unsure if this was really what she wanted to do. Her womanhood had been untouched by the outside world for so long, why lose decades of purity for a quick bunk? Her chastity was admirable, she had withheld herself longer then I had been alive. Her age was more of a factor for her than to me. She was concerned that being old enough to be my mother would be a turn off. I assured her that her age was of no consequence to me. A hole is a hole, regardless of age.

That evening I was invited over, her home just ten minutes from mine by car. I parked on the street and walked up the long stone driveway with my bag in hand. Approaching the door and knocking set off the tiny dog alarm, its yipping relentless until it knew who I was. The door opened. it was dark inside and I could only make out her face. She was not bad looking, pretty cute bubbly cheeks told me she had a few extra pounds but that was no real issue. As I stepped in I got hit with the smell.

The home was a hoarder home, not the worst I had seen but definitely in the top ten. A long skinny path is what you had to follow to get through the heap. The face had been misleading. She was not merely chubby, but rather a woman of grand proportion. Much less aroused then I was before, I contemplated just running away. I could have easily made a break for it, but that was not the right thing to do. I told her I was going to make her squirt. A man of my word, I had to at least try.

She finally reached the stairs and sat down. I was confused. Did she really expect to fuck on the stairs? A second later the chair was moving. The seat that attaches to the railing for the elderly was what she had. It sounded underpowered and made a grinding noise as she slowly disappeared up the stairwell. You have got to be fucking kidding me at this point. I suppressed a half laugh, half cry and follow behind her up to her bedroom.

The bed was the only clean thing in that room. It had become misshapen by her size but it would do. The dog had given up. It had accepted that I was here to stay and lay on the bed beside her. Her nightgown slid up to reveal what I was there for- that big meaty pussy.

I crawled between her massive thighs and got to work. Her body was not used to this kind of attention and reacted the way a virgin's would. She was so wet I had no need for gloves. Her heavy meat curtains were excited by my touch. Not long after I began, I could feel her getting close to orgasm. I increased speed, her legs trembled, her hands squeezed hard on the covers beneath, she was cumming. I continued my handiwork as she began to squirt all over the only clean spot in the room. A minute later she was done, mission accomplished.

What was I to do? I had a willing pussy in front of me, more than likely willing to accept my dick inside it. She was past the age of bearing children so I could even cum inside. The offer was a tempting one, but I just could not get over the smell in the house. The woman was clean, if only the floor had been. I took my leave after washing my hands. She offered to please me, to let me make love to her. I reminded her all we had agreed to was to teach her to squirt and that anything else would be something for another day. She smiled and waved goodbye as I made my way out. Back before I reached notch fifty I guarantee you I would have buried myself deep inside her and given that womb a fresh coat of white paint to advance my quest. Being a free man had its perks, saying no is one of them.

    Not long after that night is when my world came crashing down. March 21st, 2018 was a day that will live in infamy for those in the lifestyle. An executive order was passed with the greatest of intentions but the most horrible side effects for people in the life. FOSTA - Fighting Online Sex Trafficking Act was truly needed. People were being abused and sold online. Pimps dominated one site that ended up getting shut down by the FBI. The issue needed tackled, but what they did was take down online sex for everyone. No reputable site offered free classified ads anymore and the world will never be what it once was.

    With no more online classifieds I was left with only dating sites and various apps. I tried several but all seemed to be rigged. The majority of profiles are fake and the only way you talk to actual people is by paying money on a supposedly *free* service. I am frugal, and will not pay to talk to, meet, or hook-up with anyone. My philosophy is that love should be free, end of story.

I tried for weeks to find a woman who wanted to be pleased but came up empty handed. If I was going to have any more fun with strangers, it meant trying something new. I joined an app where it is only men looking to hook up. Perhaps they would be more willing to have fun and hopefully I could enjoy it too.

What I was hoping for and what I found were two very different things. The community was dominated by men I had no interest in. I had a type, and most of those I found online were not it or, more often than not, not interested in me in return. The amount of offers I got from tops looking to pound my bubble butt was ridiculous. Apparently I am cute in that world to muscular hairy men? It's gotta be the dimples.

A few weeks went by before I found my first willing partner. He was a virgin and very nervous about trying this. My goal was to transfer my knowledge about helping female virgins over to help male ones as well. In my eyes, this was a noble cause. I invited him over, the plan was to start off slow and only insert a butt plug this time.   I told him to go buy one for himself, he could not, for he was too scared of being judged. A man so far in the closet he couldn't even see the doorknob. I told him to bring twenty bucks, I would sell him a butt plug and install it free of charge.

When he arrived and was welcomed in I had the strongest case of deja vu. This man was a stranger to me and was visible shaking. He was nervous even though I was calm. I invited him upstairs and told him to strip down and sit on the loveseat I had for these sorts of occasions. As I clicked the door shut it clicked, *I* was once him. This situation nearly paralleled my first experience with a man. I knew exactly how he felt. Now, I *was* the old man.

Everything went smooth as he was. This man had no hair and his asshole practically sucked the butt plug out of my hand. He was relieved he did not feel the pain he was told he would feel. Had he not followed orders, that would have hurt like a son of a bitch, but he was submissive and listened. He was too submissive actually, that became the reason it ended there and we never saw each other again. He made offers to be my live in housemaid and cum slut. Even without sex, he wanted to do my laundry and my dishes. His pleasure was derived from serving and I truly wish I had that need. I would have kept him if I did.

I was only able to find one other male virgin on there. He ended up being the last guy I ever tried anything with. Living just a few hundred yards from me was a huge turn on when he replied. To find someone so close is a miracle, the opportunities to have fun increase dramatically with such a short time in travel. He was my type too, kind of on the thicker side with a nice bubble butt. His attitude is what I could not overcome.

He came over with the intent of losing his ass cherry to me. I was going to bend him over the couch and fill his virgin ass with my man meat- a simple plan in my eyes. Unfortunately it hopped off the god dam rails. He came over and came upstairs but was too nervous to go through with it. He wanted an emotional attachment to it which is something I cannot provide. I am not attracted to men, I merely hope I can pretend it's a woman and finish. A hole's a hole, right?

The nail in the coffin for him, and for the quest for men in general was (just after he chickened out and decided to leave)when he pointed across the room and asked me,"Can I have that?"

I looked over and he was pointing at ole reliable. It was standing on the table firmly attached by the suction cup at the base. I let him have it. Cannot say for sure why I just could not tell him no, but I couldn't. When he left with it, it was like losing a piece of me.

I'm not one to collect mementos. If we do not count my wife, I do not have a single pornographic image or video of anyone. Some sick people keep underwear or other treasures to remember their glory years but that is not my style. I should have kept ole reliable, like a sword she could have hung on the wall or inside a display cabinet next to this book. Out of all my experiences past and present, this is my heaviest regret. It is one of only two. The other was not putting a fresh set of batteries in that egg back in chapter twelve. As of this writing I have had sex with fifty seven women and six men. Most of these were strangers, a select few were friends. To have so few regrets after all this time is something I can live with.

CHAPTER EIGHTEEN
I am not food

    With FOSTA in full swing my old life was gone. I was like a child who had broken a vase, standing there desperately trying to glue the pieces back together and hoping no one would notice. My veil of anonymity was gone, the one true advantage I had which made me equal to everyone. I know I am not the most handsome guy on the planet, so every time I had attempted with dating sites in the past I had met with failure. I decided to give it one last attempt. I was not willing to give up everything I had come to know and love without a fight.

    The battle was intense and went on for months. Every woman was looking for Mr.Right instead of Mr.Make-me-cum. They wanted commitment over cunnilingus. More wanted fed rather then bred. Longed to be dated rather then masturbated. Swooned over spooned. You get the point. I was only able to find one girl willing to take me up on the offer. I say girl because she was still a virgin.

She was open to being bred, but first she wanted fed. Something I was more than willing to do seeing as how she was my only option. This was going to be a no pressure offer, whether she wanted to pursue a physical encounter after was entirely voluntary. She was a larger girl so I took her to the buffet. We were both large, and I can say without a doubt we got our money's worth. We chatted the whole ride out, the whole meal, and the whole ride back to her place. I dropped her off and thought that was the end of it.

A few days later she messaged me back, willing to talk more about the whole affair. I agreed and we set a plan to get breakfast again. A different buffet, a different meal, but the same outcome. She was just not looking for casual sex right now. Fine by me. As we drove back to her place somehow I managed to convince her to instead come back to mine and at the very least let me eat her pussy for a bit. I was rubbing her thigh the whole conversation to console her and make her feel like that was the right move. It was a start at least.

Having her back at my place felt like things were getting back to normal. Sure, she may not have had an amazing body but she claimed to be a virgin. I intended to verify this and if it was true, possibly hunt this down to the bitter end. What was I truly willing to do for one more virgin notch in my belt.

Undressing for her was literal torture. Even with constant reassurances she was still ashamed of her body. I showed her my erection, trying to prove any way that I could that she was worthy of love. She was a human being, more importantly a female one with a decent personality. Finally the panties hit the floor, her face was red with embarrassment as she sat down and slowly spread her thighs apart. My time to shine was now. I closed in and gently slid my finger up and down her slit. She may have been embarrassed but she was horny. The thigh rubbing I had slipped in on the ride over must have done the trick.

Before diving in with my tongue I quickly spread her open, and yes, she was a virgin. The sight of her hymen brought my urges to another level. I didn't just lick and suck the pussy before me, I worshiped it. The holy grail I was after was just inches below the surface. For thirty minutes her sex was my only target. Her moans ripped through the otherwise silent house. With every orgasm her nails dug deep into my shoulders. My face was sore as I got up and sat down beside her with a thick coating of her musk on my face. I put my hand on her thigh and turned on the TV, waiting for her to settle down and expecting nothing in return for my service. She redressed herself and as it turns out I was right. I was getting nothing in return.

The day did not end there, we cuddled on the couch and had a very interesting long talk. Her mouth ran like a broken faucet as she felt the need to show me every single picture on her social media account. Every relative, employer, and person she had ever met was now someone I magically had to know about. Did she think we were dating now or something? I cannot say for sure what was going through her mind as we sat there, learning about her past. When it came time to drop her off she was sad. She enjoyed my company now and I was still willing to tolerate hers. Before we reached the door she asked me something that no one had ever asked me.

"Hey this may sound weird, but can I bite you?" She asked, a grin across her face that to me was mildly disturbing.

"No thank you?" I replied, kind of confused by the question.

"Pity... That really would have turned me on." She said as she led the way out the door.

As I dropped her off and waved goodbye I became more and more confused by that last question. Was she really some kind of freak? Did she have a darker side that I did not yet know about? Had I upset her even?

A few days went by before she messaged me again. She wanted, you guessed it, to go out to breakfast. I told her I was looking for more then breakfast. She agreed that she would not mind having me eat her out again. As tempting an offer as that was , I implored her I was more than willing to do so but only with the agreement that she would do the same for me. She agreed, saying that she had given a blow job before and that I was in for a real treat.

Breakfast went over well and she was much less nervous about undressing now. I was the first person to see her without pants on in her entire adult life. She was twenty three, or at least claimed to be when we got together. I got to work, showing her as good a time as I had before. Her juices ran down my throat as I brought her to orgasm after orgasm. Time to find out what she could do in return. On the car ride over she had made it very clear that this was as far as she would go before marriage. No anal, no pussy, her face was my only option unless I was going to put a ring on her finger. I prayed I could make this work.

I was willing to live with the fact that we could go no further. That was not a deal breaker for I truly did respect her right to make that choice. If we simply could have traded good oral we would have been fine, but unfortunately this was not the case.

When we swapped positions I was expecting the sloppy toppy knob gobbler 3000. What I got was oral sex that could be comparable to that from a fish. It was the worst oral I have ever received. Remember chapter one where I lost blood? I much rather would have had that. At least Emily could make me finish. The refusal to use her tongue made this quite the challenge. Some time went by and she popped off. Looking up at me and squeezing tightly on my member.
"You can cum in my mouth, but only if I get to bite you after, agreed?" She knew I wanted to cum in her mouth.
"Sure, sure, just not too hard," I said, hoping she was going to crank up the heat. I was not so lucky.

Unable to take the lack of sensations I began to move her head for her, her lips the only reprieve I could feel. I was shaking her head like she was at a heavy metal concert when I finally was able to blow my load. It was massive, the lack of professionalism had edged me to the point where when the levees finally gave way, nothing would be left standing. She pulled her mouth off of me, a string of cum leaking from her lips as she bit down hard on my thigh. She locked on like a rabid dog as she bit into my tender flesh. I resisted the urge not to punch her with all god gave me. This really fucking hurt, I saw a pink creamy goo run out the side of her mouth. This bitch drew blood.

Shocked at what happened and pressing my underwear into my thigh to stop the bleeding I was beside myself. Do I yell at her for doing something I had agreed too? She got up and sat beside me, asking for a review of how she did. I lied and said it was great. I did not want to upset her and get even more holes put in me. After the bleeding stopped I got dressed and drove her home. She was happy, that mattered more to me than honesty at that moment.

That was my last time trying online dating. Although there are women on there, the hunt was not worth the take. I never did see her again, told her I just could not live with not getting her pussy. She understood but was saddened. She really liked me. Said the only taste better than my cum was my blood. Although she was the one who ended up biting into me, I was the one who bit off more then I could chew.

CHAPTER NINETEEN
Grasping at straws

Over time more and more methods seemed to prove themselves either unreliable or useless. I began to face the fact that life had changed and I was made obsolete. The only option remaining on the table was real world encounters. People I either met in person or had met in the past were all that remained. My career keeps me from having much free time to go out to a bar to meet anyone new. I went to the extreme, I left no stone unturned from my past. Over a period of weeks I tried to touch base with anyone who had flaked on me in the past. Anyone who knew me, or knew *of* me. I messaged every classmate I thought might remember my name. One person responded, just one.

To send out a literal shit storm of messages and only get one reply was truly disheartening. I knew I had burned bridges back in high school, but surely after nearly ten years I might be a different person. I was a different man back then. Back in those days, I was truly a vindictive asshole. Now however, I saw myself as just a mild asshole with good karmic intentions.

   To say we were close would be a lie. We shared a class or two back in high school and were, in general, friendly towards one another. We had a few mutual friends so we knew *of* each other. Both of us had changed since high school, my life in general was going great while she got a pretty raw deal. Monica and I were happily married and had just had our dream wedding a few months prior. My career had changed, I had gone from working in a warehouse to driving a truck. She on the other hand was barely getting by. She was raising two kids on her own. She had been made a widower when a drunk driver drove head on into her husband two years prior. Why do the good die young?

   She was grateful to hear my condolences on her loss. I was one of very few who had attempted to contact her after graduation. Perhaps the kids scared people away for she was a fairly attractive five foot five brunette. She had baby weight in all the right places. She had not been complimented in a long time. My flirting quickly won her over. I explained what my life had been after high school. She was shocked, yet curious at what I had to offer. Within days she had set up a time where her mom could watch the kids while she came over and played.

   When she arrived at my door I was in awe of how comfy she looked. She wore a loose fitting t-shirt and a snug pair of leggings with a floral pattern on them.

Her curves very visible through the fabric. I invited her in, making sure my eyes followed that sweet ass all the way to the couch. We talked for nearly an hour before anything happened. She agreed it was time to move on. Two years had been long enough.

The fact she had withheld herself for so long is truly commendable. A real woman of virtue. I handled her with the utmost respect. Like a skilled assassin I went to town on her clit. I drew out foreplay as long as I could, making sure no part was neglected. Her neck was kissed, ears nibbled, her breasts an all you can lick-suck-and fondle buffet. Her ass was smacked with ferocity. Before her clothes came off her mound was fully swollen, now visible behind the thin fabric.

I threw on a condom and slowly pounded her in several positions. A few minutes of missionary, then a few of doggy style, then I tried to finish it off in the pretzel dip. Outside I looked all powerful but inside the spirit was withered. My endurance is not the best, and after fifteen plus minutes I was ready to cum or collapse. Her pussy was a mangled mess as her moans of pleasure echoed throughout the living room. She reached down and started to play with herself.
"I know you're wearing a condom, leave it on and finish inside me. I want to feel it twitch," she said as she bit her bottom lip.

That request pumped me up more then ripping a line of booger sugar. With a renewed sense of duty I began slamming into her. She rubbed her clit faster and faster, I could feel her cumming as her pussy tried to hold me inside. She was squirting and the splashing sounds pushed me over the edge. My hips bucked one last time as I emptied my balls inside that condom. It began to leak out the base as I withdrew several moments later. I look to the sky and take a sigh of relief and as I do I feel a tugging down below. She had pulled it off and was drinking my seed. Her tongue darting in and out of the rubber lapping up every drop. She was a freak for sure.

Even after two kids her vagina had held my throbbing rod like a liquid cocoon. She laid there on the couch, fingering herself and tossing my baby butter around with her tongue. I could feel myself getting hard again. The heartbeat once again pounding in my loins.
"Well I need to be getting home, my kids need me." She said with a smile.
She dressed herself and found her way to the door, leaving me stranded and hard. This girl may have been a tease, but she was a keeper for sure. As long as things didn't get weird, we would be fine.

I had her over several more times, each time pushing her limits on how much cock she could handle. Her pussy liked the attention, after being starved for so long, who would not like it? I would drop her off at her mom's place and every single time her nipples were so hard they stuck out clear as day. She would reek of sex and on occasion she would be walking different then when she left. Her cunt was my personal gym, her cervix my heavy bag. Her mom knew, and thats when things got weird.

Perhaps women do this more then men, but to my knowledge I know of no one that talks to their parents about their sex life. My mother passed away never knowing who or what I was, what I am. My father only knows I've been with my wife and the girl from chapter six. For some reason she spilled the beans and told her mom all about us. Not what I was hoping would happen. Not a true deal breaker though, as her mom was happy her daughter was getting the dicking down of a lifetime and was much happier then she had been before I contacted her. All was well until she caught feelings.

From the very beginning I was open and honest about my marriage and that I was not looking for any emotional attachment. My goals were only physical, not emotional. After what turned out to be our final session of ground and pound she asked me to be with her. She was looking for a father figure for the kids and wanted me in her life. I politely declined, she was heartbroken. She told me I had to make a choice, I could be with her and put a baby in her or we were through. I dropped her off and we have not spoken since.

There I was with every option tapped dry. Every app, site, and past experience was thoroughly exhausted. No more loose ends to tie, no stones left unturned. My past was now truly in the past. Every experience from now on was going to have to be someone new. Someone real world who just happened to stumble across me. What was once a raging river of pussy was now down to a leaky faucet. I have only been with one other woman since (not including Monica) and it has been over a year. If it stays this way and I never taste of new fruit that would be fine by me. My hunger has truly been satisfied. Not that I would not enjoy an hors d'oeuvre, but Monica will be my main course. With her as my lover, even if she is my only lover in all my remaining years, I will still die a very happy man.

CHAPTER TWENTY
My notable failures

What defines a failure? Depending on your definition there may not be room for all my failures in this book. You may think I have already written of a failure or two. The way I am choosing to define a failure in this chapter is events that took place where neither party finished. Whether by some random chance or dumb luck, things just did not pan out. I implore you to understand that without putting these short stories of failure in the mix you're getting a misrepresentation of my past. I want you to see my failures so you can learn from them. You are more than likely never going to be in some of these situations. Consider yourself lucky.

Let's start out small. I have been tricked into riding my motorcycle over forty five minutes to a person's home. Not once, not twice, but thrice. It was before I had gotten my first notch so I did not know any better. It could have been a sick prank where some kids were watching me from inside the house. It also could have been a murderer or someone looking to rob me. Fool me once, shame on you: fool me twice, shame on me: fool me thrice, go fuck yourself asshole I'm just trying to clap some cheeks.

    Getting larger, we have a story of when I had to flat out refuse myself from sex. I met this woman at a gas station as she had directed me to. She was a large Jamaican woman who wanted me to fuck her. The things she wanted done to her were beyond my physical capacity. This woman, who had to be damn near three bills if not over, wanted to be treated like a rag doll. I was supposed to hold her in the air while we fucked. My heart was telling me no, but my body - yes my body, was also telling me no fucking way.

    Stepping it up another notch was the time I fell for a sting operation with the police. I had a cute blonde message me and say she wanted to fuck. Sure why the hell not? The onlynly issue was she was quite far away. I drove forty five minutes to the address I was given. I sat in the driveway and immediately I was suspicious. Every light was on in the house, typically no lights were on in the places I went. Discretion was desired by most, why would she want to advertise my arrival to her neighbors? I left my bag on the seat and went to the door. Three knocks later she answered and invited me in.

    Things were just not adding up. It was silent inside, no TV or radio on. No laptop in sight or computer. No pictures on the walls even, no family photos. We began to talk and she said she was not the person messaging me, her ex boyfriend must be playing tricks on her. If this was true, and I was not invited then why would she let a complete stranger in her house at nine thirty at night?

We talked and apparently she was on the online classifieds, but she was a pay-to-play lady. She worked for, " roses" , and demanded two hundred before we began. I told her the truth, that I would never pay for sex. I offered to eat her out and not get anything in return, she declined and showed me the door. As I got into my car I noticed a van. Two driveways down that looked totally out of place. How obvious can you be? Even the lights were on inside it. I was being watched, this was a sting and I thank god I did not take the bait.

My greatest…some would say *failure*, some would say *success*, was at a glory hole. I had only ever seen them in movies up until that night and what I saw seemed to fit the bill quite well. The only picture in the ad was a piece of plywood with a hole in it blocking a doorway. Don't fix what ain't broken.

The ad was run by a couple that wanted a man to come over and join the husband at the glory hole. No male on male play, just take turns having fun with the woman on the other side. A decent enough proposition, I thought it was kinky so I replied. Within the hour I was heading over.

The husband let me in. He was quite handsome and his wife looked awful cute sitting on the couch. He ordered her to go get ready as we both went out on the porch to discuss logistics. He also needed a smoke before we started. I do not smoke so I try not to judge, but this guy was a fucking chain smoker. Even though he was smoking out front when I walked up, he wanted another one before we started. Fine by me, smoke em' if you got em'. We come up with a plan, I get first use of the hole and then he takes over once I'm done. If I want I can stick around for round two if shes willing.

So I go in there and all I see is an eye looking at me through the hole. A lone finger pokes through and ushers me in. I am only at like sixty percent when I shove myself through. She had to have a hot drink over there for her mouth was excessively warm. The sensation sent shivers down my spine as I rocked my hips forward to give her more access to me. The tongue tornado swirled around me, I began to get close to orgasm. I felt her lick the precum oozing out of me. I didn't even mind the guy staring at me from across the room and playing with himself. It was his house, his wife, his plywood. I heard him grunt and turned to see him shooting his load all over the carpet. Even that kind of turned me on. I was getting to my breaking point when his raspy voice broke through the air.
"I'm gonna go have a smoke, you two have fun." He said walking back out to the porch.

I stood on my tip toes and forced as much of myself into her mouth as I could. Every time I got close to busting she would pop off and lightly play with me using her hands. This teasing bitch better have a towel back there was all I could think of. I was a hair's breadth from blowing my load when once again she popped off, this time to ask me something.

"Hey, do you wanna fuck me in the ass? I love getting fucked in the ass!" She asked, her hand still sliding up and down my cock.

"Sure, I would love that," I replied.

A squirt noise was heard as I felt cold lube being rubbed onto me. Her hands felt different with the lube. It still felt good but it was definitely different. My cock was sore and my balls ached from the edging. I knew her ass would make me bust in seconds but I didn't care. I had not gotten to see my prize at all. I heard a rustling as she repositioned herself on the other side. I felt a slight pressure on the head of my cock before I pulled it back onto my side, it was glistening with lube and bright red. The vein was trying desperately to flow even more blood inside.

"I want to see your cute little asshole before I fuck it, it helps my imagination," I say, standing back and looking down through the hole.

A cute ass is pressed up against the wood. Hands are pulling apart the cheeks to reveal a bright pink hole dead center.

"Satisfied?" She asks.

"Sure am," I say.

Had I not been at the exact angle at that exact second I never would have seen it. This perfectly shaved cute little ass was not the wife's, it was the husband's. As *"she"* pulled away I saw the beginnings of a scrotum. Had they been upfront about this from the start I would have happily came inside his ass. Now that I was being tricked, I was no longer aroused. You're going to have to wake up pretty early to get me with the ole hot swap trick.

"Actually, Its getting pretty late. I should be heading home. Thank you for the good time." I said, stuffing my lube-covered swollen fuck stick back in my pants and making a dash for the door.

I heard her yell, "Wait don't go!" This was followed by her husband asking "How did he fucking know?"

I jogged back to car and sped off. They tried emailing me but I did not write back. I pulled over along the side of the highway and put my four ways on. I found a fast food bag in the back seat and grabbed it. The napkins were used to clean off the lube. I was still swollen and needed to cum. I leaned my seat back and gave myself a quick tug. I busted in the fast food bag and used the last of the napkins to wipe myself clean. Not my proudest wank.

They emailed me for days, begging for me to come back. Apparently I had been the only one willing to fall into their trap. I felt pride in knowing that I only got tricked a bit. I could tell it was the wife up until a certain point. So less then sixty seconds of a handy was all that guy was able to get from me before I wised up. Surprisingly this has not fully scared me away from glory holes and, if given the opportunity, I would be willing to try again in the future. By giving up it would be like letting them win. Refuse to let someones abuse ruin your opportunities in life, they can only truly hurt you if you let them.

CHAPTER TWENTY-ONE
What's left for me

    Your options in life are only limited by your courage and exploratory nature. Your destiny constantly altered by your actions or lack thereof. With each passing day you gain wisdom and a new perspective on your own situation. Take risks only if you can handle any of the possible outcomes.

    So what happens to me?
    Your guess is as good as mine to be honest. I went through hell and back to know deep down I was a man, but along the way learned there's more to life then tapping strange. No amount of notches can teach you courage or self respect, that can only come from within. Countless hours had been spent in pursuit of sins of the flesh. I had given sweat, tears, and even blood. Nightmares still haunt me from time to time. I have only the two previously mentioned regrets. I carry no shame for what I have done. Pride? Not quite proud, more like privileged.

    Would I do it all again?

You bet your sweet ass I would. I met my soulmate along with a bunch of other wonderful people. I've experienced bodily sensations most will never come to know. I have mastered my craft to be the best lover I can be for my wife. Although I never contracted a sexually transmitted disease, my sex life has had me seek medical care more then once. For a while I had orgasmic cyphalgia, a condition the doctor had to look up just like I did. Every time I would orgasm I would be greeted with a splitting headache. I slowed down on the sex for a while and it went away (thank god). I also have had epididymal hypertension "blue balls". That was a much easier cure for me, just have more sex and it goes away. To this day I cannot go more then two days without release or I am racked with pain.

Throughout the book you got small excerpts of my father's shortcomings throughout my life. My mother, god rest her soul, was not perfect either. We were never really as close as we should have been. She kept herself emotionally distant. The amount of happy memories I have of her can be counted on just my fingers.

Her efforts could be described as the bare essentials to being a mother. She was more likely to be found smoking a bowl than cleaning one. Overall only one trauma seems to stick out in my mind. Laundry fell behind quite often and clean underwear became a commodity. In times of shortage I was forced to wear my sister's underwear. I begged and pleaded but my efforts were fruitless. I was given the "If they would catch you without underwear on at school they would think I'm a bad mother," on more then one occasion. I spent those days terrified that someone may find me out. A bright pink whale tail would mean the end of me. What little friends I was able to make would surely no longer associate themselves with a cross dresser.

In case that message was not crystal clear, DO NOT do that to your child.

A second thing to not do to your child, do not shit all over their career choice. As a young boy. I desired very much to be a mechanic. I loved the thought of working on cars. The dream was to run my own shop and make decent money. Both of my parents disagreed. Every time they got that answer they made me feel ashamed the words escaped my lips. Any future child I have, whether they want to be the president or a prostitute, has my full support. I do not care about their income or career prospects, I care only for their happiness.

A third thing not to do to your child, do not try and guide them down a particular path of sexual preference. My mother tried to sway my sister as my father tried to sway me. The level of misogyny was barbaric. I was more disgusted than encouraged. We love who we love.

On the topic of sex, please please please talk to your kids about sex. Emily and I were only thirteen when we first got together so you may want to have the talk at twelve. Teach them how to properly use a condom so when the time comes they can be safe. Encourage abstinence but understand that if telling someone not to do something bad actually worked then all the rehabs and prisons would go out of business. School had taught me nothing that proved useful. I did not know how to get, buy, or use a condom. I am very lucky I am not a father.

A good practice would be to let them know that you love them and want them to be safe. Do not in any way encourage the adult behaviors, but provide a safety net for them if they choose to do so.

Who I was, who I am, and who I will become are all in the eye of the beholder. You may have viewed me as a man who changed or the same asshole from chapter one. I could be viewed as curious and open, or I could be a dirty pervert. I personally see an evolution in human decency and kindness but I'm biased. A racist homophobic asshole ends up marrying a black woman and does not mind when he gets fucked in the ass. I see a definite change there.

You truly can change your self if you put your mind to it. Throughout life people will try and change you either for the better or the worse and it's up to you how you evolve. Faith is a strong topic of conversation in my career and there is no shortage of people looking to convert you to their way of thinking.

A year or so before writing this book I finally decided to open up about my life to some co-workers.

After hearing just the tip of the iceberg they wanted me to come to Christ. The seed Mr.G had planted several years ago was now getting water and light. JF and LS were the ones who wanted to bring me to Christ. I had my doubts and knew nothing of that world. I insisted before I made a decision that I would read the book.

That journey of reading the book took sixty eight hours for me to read cover to cover. Fifteen months of reading in my spare time to learn that although I do believe the story to be true, I see not a way in which I can align myself with the ideals of the lord. If society was as it was when the book was written I believe I would be fine. If I could marry multiple people and form a harem, I honestly would. I cannot feel repentant for actions I committed only because societal law and gods law are two different laws. I will continue to work through my struggles and may become repentant in time. For now I remain in the darkness even though I was shown the light.

That spiritual quest lead me to read the Quran as well. I highly recommend you read that cover to cover. Everything you have probably heard about it is wrong. Women are treated much better and that's something I can respect. Look to the book, not the followers. Priests molesting children should not alter the message of the new testament just as misguided terrorists should not alter the message of the Quran.

The shocking thing is most people of faith base their eternity on a few choice phrases hand selected from a book by a person *whose job it is* to make you believe. The good book has been around for longer then most. Understand if people talk about a book for centuries it's probably worth a read, just my opinion.

People like me are out there, no different from yourself. Every person that I have showed a section of this book too prior to release has been shocked at what was in the pages. Our families are still blissfully unaware of our lifestyle and we do hope and pray it stays that way. If you know us in real life, take our secret to your grave.

For those who know us not, perhaps I am the bouncer at the night club you just got done dancing at or telemarketer who just called trying to sell you something you will never need. Is it more likely that I am the mover you hired or the humble milkman driving down a country lane? People like me exist, we are everywhere. Love us and accept us for who we are and the world can be a better place.

If you enjoyed reading this book please go on amazon and give it a review. Do the same if you hated it. Let the world know if you learned a lesson or had a good laugh. Tell them how you cried, or how you were wet elsewhere. ail:

Humbly Yours,
Rick Labour